DEAD WRONG

ISBN: 978-1-7359803-9-3

DEAD WRONG

J. EVERETT DUTSCHKE

SEPTEMBER 11, 2001

. . .

FRUSTRATING. THAT WAS THE word which best described Rett's life at the moment. Sure, other people probably have their troubles, but it really seemed to Rett that everyone around him was happy with how things were going in their lives.

Rett James's good friend, Michael Noel, was engaged to an amazing southern belle, Jenny, and Mr. Noel's taekwondo school was small, but the students active and loyal. Noel and Jenny seemed happy with each other.

Why couldn't Rett have some of that?

Everything just felt like tragedy on the verge of disaster. Not much was going right.

Just a few months before, Rett had taken his wife, a multimillionaire's daughter, to a satellite industry expo in Hollywood. Hollywood, Florida, that is. Satellite business owners, CEOs, lobbyists, technicians, and even programming representatives and contract companies hobnobbed with each other.

Some guests had already made news or a name for themselves in the industry. A young guy named Mark Cuban was there, who'd just sold his company, HDNet, for over a billion dollars. What would the young man end up doing with that amount of money? Larry King was there, probably promoting CNN. Different channels sent celebrities to promote those channels (including the Playboy Channel, who sent Jessica Drake and some other smart blonde). Jeff Foxworthy was the hired entertainer one night ("You might be a redneck"). During the white tablecloth banquet and dance, the frivolity was led by the B-52s ("Love Shack"). And billionaire CEO Charlie Ergan tried to act generous and humble in the face of it all. He is, really. Funny how that works, the blue-collar, newly-made billionaires all seem to actually be really nice guys, more into what they do rather than what they're worth. The money came as a secondary reward.

Rett James was like that.

Minus the billion dollars, of course.

But he'd taken steps to get there. Or, so he thought.

Capitalizing on the forced sale of Wireless One, a wireless cable company liquidated by the failing Mississippi-based telecom company named WorldComm, Rett found a way to finance his own start-up—which he hoped to build into a billion-dollar monster.

The internet was the big thing and everyone was on it, or getting there. Every town now boasted at least three or four internet service providers, each vying for new subscribers.

Not that a local ISP was the only choice. Just as many people signed up with Earthlink or AOL, or some other overnight multibillion-dollar company, just because of their ubiquitous configuration CD-ROMs available for free in Wal-Marts, supermarkets, and even inserted in magazines.

But Rett James had used his telecom connections, drive,

motivation, and intellect (as well as nearly every available penny) to offer what even the multibillion monsters couldn't.

High-speed internet.

eLocity was his new baby and was to revolutionize the world. No longer would subscribers need to dial up a number on their phone line, tying it up to slowly receive or load photos, websites, or compressed music (MP3s). With eLocity, Rett James could delight customers with downloads in mere seconds, not minutes.

The local ISPs couldn't do that. Neither could AOL or the other big boys. Rett had invested in R&D, technical engineering, software development, and a small amount of beta testing in targeted markets where he'd already opened and staffed offices of salespeople, managers, and installers ready to go—primarily in the South, where access to T1 or fiber-optic would not be available for at least a decade. Cities like Tupelo, Laurel, and Jackson in Mississippi; Huntsville, Alabama; Williamsburg, Virginia; and Boston, Massachusetts.

This was satellite internet. Well, kind of.

At the satellite industry conference in Florida, Rett James had revealed what he'd been building—eLocity. A hybrid system which utilized dial-up to send information out—uploads—and a medium-sized satellite dish and a custom-installed satellite modem to receive information—downloads.

The speed at which it worked (when it functioned properly) made customers say "Wow!" Rett's people even sold the idea (bold for 2001) that live audio and unbuffered live video would be ubiquitous in people's homes. Not that people thought that such content would ever really be available, but eLocity staff were tossing out new words like 'streaming' to describe it to dubious prospects and customers.

Rett loved to see, visibly, the 'Wow!' wash over a customer. This was his billion-dollar hope—a side gig that he'd developed into a viable major telecom, while working a main gig that soon would become just the side gig.

In 2001, he was but a young man when he'd made his major deal with Qwest and launched his iSat platform. The future should be bright.

He needed it to be bright.

His wife was the daughter of a multimillionaire financier who detested his daughter's choice to be with 'mystery man' Rett James. Rett would never join the tycoon's religion or set one foot in that church. Nor would he join up with the family business the way all the other Washington family sons-in-law did when marrying into the family.

Unlike the others, Rett was not interested in the Washington millions. Rett James would make his own. Hell, he'd spent nearly that much in readying eLocity for the market.

But then came the convention in Florida.

It was there that another satellite executive began to unravel the hard-working dream that was eLocity when he personally showed Rett that the multibillionaire Charlie Ergan had made a deal which would render eLocity obsolete. The industry moves fast. Failure to not only keep up but keep ahead equals plain failure. Ergan's product was a high-speed satellite system which was both up and downlink via sat dish and modem. No phone line needed.

And Ergan wasn't the only one. Satellite television provider DirectTV, a true giant, was releasing DirectPC at that time, which also had a direct two-way sat-link option.

In addition to the massive technological head start of Ergan's Echosphere and DirectTV's DirectPC, those two media giants also had a massive marketing head start over Rett James's eLocity.

They did not need to go out and pound the pavement to locate a customer base. They already had an existing subscriber base of mostly suburban and rural households to market to. Rett, conversely, would have to turn over every rock in the country against those two giants.

Rett had also made an early R&D decision which would be devastating—opting for the design of an internal-expansion-card-installed sat modem.

The rationale was simply that it was a cleaner install, not some external box as an extra desk accessory that Rett thought people simply wouldn't like. His installers would literally open a new subscriber's desktop and physically install the eLocity modem card, which was coax connected to a dish outside. Plus, Rett thought, having that custom modem card inside one's computer makes that customer feel more long-term committed. A stickier customer.

That too was a mistake. As it turns out, there was no trend against external accessory boxes. In fact, the other companies put extra lights on their external modems just because it tested with focus groups as some sort of positive.

So Rett's hopes (along with absurd amounts of money) were fading fast and he needed a massive influx of cash to redesign and manufacture the new technology he'd need to be competitive enough to gain the quarter-million customers he'd need just to position eLocity for sale. At which point, one of the two big guys—maybe Ergan, maybe Hughes—would buy him out just for the paper (which means for the subscribers, not the technology).

But getting that kind of money was getting harder every day.

It's not like his other job was going to help that much. There's not a lot of money in the odd contract for payload telemetry these days. Plus, those satellite launches were becoming less frequent and his bizarre, sometimes last-minute absences did not help with Rett's attention to his own company or attention to his attention-starved wife, Anita.

He had incorporated Anita into as much of his life as he could, his lifelong and daily training and teaching of taekwondo, the satellite business, even his family (to a small degree). He'd even permanently moved to Tupelo, simply because of her. But his odd-timed flights, spending a few days away, never sat well with her. When he'd attend a new launch, often as far away as Kazakhstan, he'd return home to a sullen, depressive, and suspicious woman and learn that she hadn't left the house, but stayed in bed, often forgetting to even eat for a week.

Well, success changes things. Even relationships. Once Rett could reach the financial level he wanted, well, she'd come around. That's how that worked, right? The issues in the relationship had to be his fault, right? Her standard of living was a high bar as set by her insanely wealthy father, a level Rett James couldn't reach. But he had to. And he had to on his own. The problems couldn't be because she is bipolar and completely crazy. After all, he'd always had a real weakness for crazy chicks. Doesn't every man?

The launch telemetry contracts were the remaining vestiges of an intelligence operation for the CIA that wasn't really bearing much fruit these days—not in terms of good intel on other countries' or companies' launched payloads, nor financially for Rhett. In fact, it's easy to lose money that way, since he had to bid low to get each job done.

When it rains, it pours. And it was currently a steady shower of bad fortune about to get worse.

One of the bulbs (Anita insisted on only 40-watters) in the master bath was out. Because Anita had insisted on full-fledged, tasseled, platinum-trimmed royal drapery (in layers) instead of a simple, single opaque shower curtain (Rett would be fine shopping at a dollar store), it was dark inside the shower itself this Tuesday morning.

"It figures," Rett muttered, entering the shower. "One more example of something in my life only working half-assed. Can I depend on anything?!?"

Starmaxx, the company Rett had created to fulfill the launch telemetry contracts, was not going to rescue him. Part of Rett's plan was to take on an additional contract needed by the Agency's Technical Service in which Rett would open and ghost-staff multiple 'businesses' in supporting the Central Cover Office. Like the Starmaxx contract, it wouldn't pay a ton, but it would be well within Rett's experience.

But now, even *that* possibility was looking grim.

Rett was pretty sure he was about to be fired and blacklisted.

Tomorrow morning, he was scheduled for a meeting with the Agency's OPI (Office of Procurement Integrity). When OPI gets around to a personally scheduled meeting, they already have their minds made up. And even if they didn't drop the axe immediately, they'd initiate a chain of events that would lead to it.

One thing the CIA of 2001 wouldn't tolerate was misallocation or misappropriation of funds. Even though Rett was sure that the specific thing they'd accuse him of wasn't true, they'd end up scheduling him for the box (a polygraph exam) which would lead to a few lines of questioning—resulting in a few what's-the-big-deal kind of answers. He'd become a hall-walker in limbo for months before the axe fell.

And it isn't like Rett James had a lot of political capital these days, since he wasn't exactly one of the star recruits of the Directorate of Operations (DO). He wasn't even a blue-card Case Officer (C/O) anymore. Green badge contractors don't usually have to do that stuff. Not that Rett hadn't. He certainly had. And his recruited agents were very valuable and generally not only *knew* things, but could *do* things. From Rett's point-of-view, operational assets are ten times more valuable than the celebrated intelligence assets. (That's why he frequently kept them in his own network rather than an official handoff.) That was in the past; the CIA is a what-have-you-done-for-me-lately kind of business.

The corridors and vaults of the headquarters at Langley were filled with self-congratulating men and women, all too eager to pat themselves on the back for their many silent victories—giving themselves awards and commendations (which no one will ever see) for simply doing their jobs, while simultaneously completely missing something somewhere else. The Langley-bound analysts, administrators, and in-house support had hardly any real appreciation at all for the near-miracles performed in the field, though no one would admit it.

This is why the average career span in the DO was five to six years (before a dramatic change) as opposed to the analysts of the DI, who often enjoy 30–35 years at Langley. The worst day for an analyst might be that someone has taken a favorite parking spot on the third-tier deck (the south corners of the top tier are rarely occupied), the Starbucks might mix up his order (unlike other Starbucks, the Agency Starbucks doesn't write names on cups) or his burn bag might pop open (always use four staples).

By contrast, the worst day for anyone in the field—whether Directorate of Operations (DO) or Technical Services (TS)— is incomprehensible and not even relatable. Rett James had not had one of those moments yet.

This is the backdrop of *that* moment.

FOG?

• • •

As Rett James adjusted the shower's temperature and aimed Anita's overly complicated, multi-setting shower head for a normal-sized person (Anita is only 5'2"), he mentally re-inventoried everything he'd packed into his suitcase, which was sitting on the bed—zipped up and ready for his late evening flight to D.C. (from Memphis to Dulles).

"Suh LYOG him parom," Rett muttered in Russian when the temperature was right, then reached for the Dial bar soap—difficult to find amongst Anita's forest of scented bottles of… whatever it all is. One of the saddest things to recognize about Americans is that if they cannot display copious vessels of fragrant, multicolored, enhancing broths in their showers like pageant trophies or wipe their butts with scented cotton candy, then the American Dream has somehow betrayed them.

Within a few minutes, he heard the cracked bathroom door pushed aside and Anita's curious voice announce, "A plane just hit the World Trade Center!"

Odd. "Manhattan?"

"Yes," Anita answered.

"Hmm," was Rett's only response.

Rett's father had once been a pilot. The World Trade Center is immensely big. It would be really hard for any pilot to fail to notice such an immense pair of buildings.

"Fog?" Rett asked, trying to figure it out. "Rain?"

"No," Anita answered. "Crystal clear day."

Rett knew Fox News had been on in the bedroom, the morning show is in Manhattan—so they'd know.

It must have been a small plane, Rett thought. *Serious engine trouble. Planes in trouble do hit buildings from time to time. I wonder if the pilot or his passenger survived*, Rett found himself thinking out of nothing but hope.

Meanwhile, his thoughts turned to his own predicament. If he was to be fired tomorrow, how would he tell Anita? It was a passing question, really. He knew his nature. He knew he wouldn't tell her anything. Otherwise, he'd have to tell her everything. It would have to suffice to just tell her the meeting didn't go well, then remind her that he had money problems.

This was not an easy thing to say to a wife. Particularly so with a wife who is the daughter of a multimillionaire. Money troubles are something you keep to yourself, then work to fix. You certainly don't advertise it.

Plus, it's a huge red flag to the CIA. One whiff of that and the Office of Security (OS) starts inquiries and you're called in for a 'random' polygraph. It certainly wouldn't help with the OPI inquiry, that's for sure.

"Misallocation of Agency resources?"

You may as well just say "stealing!" No truth to that at all!

"Maybe if my requests weren't met with an automatic no, then I wouldn't need to find creative ways of procuring or spending. I told you people I needed some things done.

You shouldn't have told me no when I asked. So I stopped asking and found the back door! Honestly."

Maybe simply saying the honest thing would be the best approach. Probably not. Rett would have to face it. There was just not going to be an easy way out.

"Hey," Anita's voice reentered through the steam and cut Rett's ruminations short.

"Another plane just hit the World Trade Center!"

HOPING

...

Holy shit!

"You're probably just seeing them rerun some footage or repeat the story," Rett offered, hoping.

"No. I'm not! Another plane. A second plane just hit the World Trade Center. It exploded!"

Holy shit!

"We're under attack."

TURN AROUND

...

RETT AND ANITA, EMPTY and overwhelmed both, sat glued to the television. Buildings burned. People jumped. More planes were missing. In D.C., the Secretary of Defense literally pulled injured, bleeding people from the rubble of the Pentagon. The White House and Capitol were evacuated. One tower fell. Another plane became wreckage in Pennsylvania. The second tower crashed down. The mayor of New York was trapped underground. The plumes of smoke and wreckage could be seen from space. Everything in the air anywhere over the U.S. was being grounded. A third tower, part of the now-feeble World Trade Center's very foundation, also fell. Footage from distant places showed celebrations in the streets. Footage from everywhere showed shock, horror, utter despair.

"I gotta go," Rett finally announced while quickly emptying a strawberry-banana yogurt with an oversized spoon.

"There are no planes. Your flight's cancelled," Anita blankly stated.

"I'll drive," Rett told her. "Listen, fill up every gas can we have and every gas tank. I'll drive the Fiero. Fill up the Expedition. The Blazer. I'll leave the Cherokee here. Fill them all up. Gas is going to go through the roof. Fill up everything. I—I don't know what else to tell you."

"You're going to drive the Fiero? To D.C.?!?"

"Sure. I can do it. In fact, that's where I bought it. Drove it all the way from D.C. to Meridian. I can deal with that. Better gas mileage than the Cherokee, too, I'll bet. You just fill up everything."

Cell phone service was spotty. And it wasn't long before it switched to roaming.

North to I-40, hang right. East on 40 to 95. Then left on 95. 95 to 495 to George Washington Parkway to Langley. The directions are simple enough. Who knows how well this tiny, overpowered two-seater will hold up?

Just around midnight—no, wait, now 1:00 the next morning, since it was around Chattanooga—Rett was finally able to reach the right person, his division director.

Normally, Rett tended to operate with a great deal of autonomy, but at the moment, he was clueless as to what to do. All he knew was it would be an all-hands-on-deck situation.

"I'm on I-40 right now," Rett informed his division director. "Headed toward Langley."

"Turn around," was all he was told. "Your agency sponsor says get your team to Colorado Springs."

"But, I'm almost there! I'll reach D.C. in a few hours. I'm almost in Virginia already."

"No you're not. Besides, your team needs to help out SCS. Can you guys do that?"

"SCS?" Rett balked as his tiny sports car was practically squashed between two massive 18-wheelers (practically the only vehicles on the highway).

"Why can't the NSA handle their own shit?!?"

"Now's definitely not the time to—"

"You're right, man. You're right. Colorado Springs it is, then. Damn. That's clear on the other side of the country. Where are we going after that?"

"I don't know," was the answer. "Might be Dearborn."

"Okay." Rett understood. He disagreed with it. Dearborn, Michigan was definitely *not* foreign, therefore whatever domestic thing Rett's CIA-contracted thing was about to do would be very illegal—but at that moment, who cared?

Within 48 hours, the shock, fear, and disbelief of the entire nation quickly faded into anger. Resolve.

Resolute vengeance.

I KNOW A GUY...

• • •

HALFWAY—KIND OF—BEFORE COLORADO, THE glowing red muffler of the rear engine (or, 'mid,' if you prefer) sports car fell off suddenly and without warning. ('Without warning' may not be entirely fair since it was a Fiero, quite known for their supernova-type events from their inferno engine compartments. However, no Fiero was designed to run this hard for this long.)

From that point forward, each cylinder combustion of the six cylinders shuddered the car as if it was being pelted by .50 caliber machine gun rounds. It was louder and more violent than a Harley on a dirt road. Despite the noise, Rett connected with Steven Belvin.

"Egg!" Rett shouted into his Nokia, over the noise.

"Are you at war, man?" Belvin asked, hearing the Fiero's racket.

"No," Rett said, then explained the situation.

"We going to war?" Egg then asked.

"I—I don't see how we can't be," Rett answered. Then, "Listen, my guys are gonna be tasked with something domestic for a bit. Sounds like busy work to me. But everyone feels compelled to do—something. Even if we don't know what."

"What do you need me to do, man?"

Okay. Here it is. "Egg—you, uh—you still know any Cicada guys?"

Silence.

Rett prodded. "Egg?"

More silence.

"What makes you think I'd know anyone like that?"

"C'mon, Egg—I'm not stupid. You're not in trouble. No one's gonna look at you. This isn't about you. I just want to tap every resource I can. Do something useful, you know?"

More silence.

Then—"I know a guy or two."

"Who's the best?"

"Mark. An Aussie."

"Okay—there were some guys living in Nashville. They had high-speed service, but then recently cancelled. They all lived together in the same house, no women, no families. They all went to the same mosque. They vanished about two weeks ago. We tried to collect the cancellation fee from their debit card, but it wouldn't go through. Their account may be shut down."

"Arabs?" Egg asked.

"Yes," Rett answered. "There's gonna be a lot of scrutiny on people like that. All of them. If you have that debit card number, do you think your Cicada buddy can do me a COI analysis on that account? They've probably donated to their mosque, which would lead to other accounts. Hundreds of them. Everyone who attends that mosque and everyone who that mosque attends to, domestic and foreign."

"I'll bet he can do that in his sleep. I suppose you want me to scrub the domestic stuff and detail anything foreign for your people?"

"Actually Egg, scrub nothing. I think we are at a point where we don't care. If I get in trouble, then I get in trouble. Get it all. Everything. I'll submit whatever interesting thing gets mined. Once we start pulling on that thread, it will lead to something. Those networks, they only seem insular. They're not. They're all connected. So… mine it all. I'll submit whatever we get. Feel like I'm—we—are actually doing something positive."

"But—"

"Don't worry, Egg. I protect my sources. I'll keep your name out of it. Call LaShaunda at my office. She'll get you that debit card number. Then approach your guy. Given all that's going on, he'll understand. Hell, he may be expecting a call. Aussie or not, he may want to help. But he may feel as helpless as—as we do."

"Okay," Egg replied. Then silence. Then—"Rett?"

Rett could hear the seriousness in Egg's voice and responded, "Yes, Egg?"

Egg's voice was shaky as the Fiero—"Did—did you guys know?"

Rett choked up and tears welled instantly.

"No, Egg," he told him. "We didn't know."

BOOM FACTOR

· · ·

RETT AND TWO FELLOW team members did end up spending a few days in Dearborn. The data collected for SCS was probably useless, but it was done anyway. The target, itself, was probably a good idea, though. Dearborn is practically under Sharia law already, thick with Muslims now looking over their shoulders.

Rett hadn't been fond of the quickie assignment. It seemed more like an afterthought and reactive. Clean-up. That's the kind of stuff left to law enforcement, and the NSA didn't seem to mind helping the FBI at all. Ever.

But that's not what Rett wanted to do. He'd never been a clean-up guy. Not CIA's mission either, though within days, that also started to turn.

For half a decade now, CIA officers and affiliates of all kinds were languishing and searching for purpose. Lying to people, framing them, bribing them to 'betray' their country 'in order to save it' had become a stale game producing little fruit. While Rett, himself, was still working on Agency-sponsored—no, make that Agency-*interested* projects (which he'd kind of been told shouldn't be worked)—and even *that* was very slow developing.

Recruitment had been low, burn-out high, and results nominal at best. Morale was flat. The DO was dwindling in relevance. The whole of foreign intel gathering was a lackluster affair. Those in the field had been getting smug, complacent, and fat.

9/11 would have an effect on everyone at the CIA. It was a wakeup call. It was a spark needed to ignite the docile flickers of interest into a burning inferno of determination. It was also a shock to the system (as it should have been), as the analysts in particular asked themselves and each other, "How the fuck did we miss this?"

Rett feared the analysts (DI) would blame those in the field (DO) actually doing the gathering, but he was sure that when it all settled, that they'd discover that the information had been gathered (or enough of it) and fed into the Intelligence Community (IC) machine, that the pieces could have all been assembled into a high-probability picture. But then, maybe it was a collection failure. Rett doubted it, but he had been wrong before.

Hell, he was way off on the initial effect on gas prices. They actually went rapidly down and as quickly as 9/12.

But the 9/11 effect on the CIA awakened a fierce determination to every affiliated man and woman. Suddenly, everyone was on board, giving 110%.

That was the problem.

Despite the near-immediate personnel surge (Rett lost two of his most reliable guys in the post-9/11 surge since everyone with military experience, like those two, were re-tasked), there really wasn't much to do.

As the CIA began to set aside its traditional espionage

mission to quickly morph into a hyper-specialized military branch, those divisions, branches, and offices that had been used for technical or Tactical Operational Support Activities (though TOSA is more of a military label) got lost in the shuffle.

Contractors, or contractors of contractors, began to rethink and repurpose their role in support of the new mission—which was primarily the hunting of men.

Just as the FBI (and other law enforcement) began hunting (and in some cases, baiting, staging, framing, and entrapping) anyone here in the homeland that they could label as a 'terrorist' in order to keep their 'score' high enough to make it appear as though they were helping, the CIA was actually working magic in the field, quietly but effectively—and with a network of allied countries.

The global reaction was profound. Countries went to extremes to help, or just as often pretended to in order to curry favor.

This is how the Macedonian Fiasco happened. But that is another story for another day. (Lesson there—every country's law enforcement apparatus, each of them, is corrupt. Not just the U.S.)

Not long after 9/11, the anthrax attacks happened. FBI director Bob Mueller found an innocent target and offered him up as the sacrificial lamb, as is the Mueller trademark. ("Who cares that he's innocent, as long as we can make him look guilty?") Because Mueller's victim, now blamed for the anthrax attacks, was a government employee who had actually been working on high-level, treaty-violating projects, the corrupt FBI machine knew the patsy wouldn't actually be allowed to talk about his work or defend himself in court. The pressure of the false prosecution, and utter destruction that the FBI usually leaves in its wake, caused the man's 'suicide' before he could talk to the press.

Convenient. The Mueller FBI closed the case, claiming it was resolved when their now-forever-silent accused prematurely expired.

Still, there was a great deal of anxiety over potential weaponization of biological agents as the next terror attack (in part because everyone with at least half a brain recognized that Mueller and the FBI were either entirely inept, or callous liars, or both). That's why Rett James, early on, penned a white paper (an analytical work product) entitled, "The Boom Factor." It was written with great conviction and detailed exactly why biological and chemical weapons would be inadequate for (therefore, not as useful as) a true terror attack, therefore the 'bioterrorism' fears were unfounded and vastly amplified for the sake of sensationalism. This would actually be more harmful to a country than such an attack, itself. Thus, classifying chemical or biological weapons as a terrorist tool is a mistake.

The paper clearly identified three key things (because most policy makers are lawyers and lawyers can't count very high):

A. Biological weapons require a vector of some sort and an agent which is contagious enough to spread to a new vector. While such a thing can cause damage and death, the only agents contagious/lethal enough to do such a job are uncontrollable (not focused enough) when released and also take time to develop. Terrorists are trying to make a statement. A slow-rolling contagion isn't an exclamation point! It is an ellipsis—which is not bold. It doesn't fit their psychology. In short, a slow-developing pandemic which is uncontrollable has no 'Boom Factor.'

B. Chemical weapons are not easy to manufacture and are not easy to deploy, like in the movies. The only chemical agents that are lethal enough and controllable enough are those which can be specifically targeted. Deployed against an individual, silently so, as for targeted assassination. This lacks the mass-casualty and/or dramatic and sudden event which makes the statement. It also isn't an exclamation point [!]. In fact, it is often (as targeted assassinations are) more of a question mark [?]. So again, it doesn't fit the psychology. No 'Boom Factor.'

C. Any attempt by any major organization, network, state, or non-state group to manufacture and/or deploy either A or B as a terrorist weapon could be very easily sabotaged.

Rett's thesis then went on to describe some hypotheticals of that ease of sabotage.

That last one (C) proved later to have been a tactical mistake by Rett to have included in the thesis, because exactly such an organization was at that moment trying to develop a chemical agent of assassination into a mass-casualty weapon on the other side of the planet and did trigger exactly such a sabot (against the aerosolization of ricin).

And who do you suppose was instrumental in coordinating such a sabotage operation (if it happened, hypothetically, of course)? Hint: It wasn't the Swiss Guard. It wasn't the Vatican. It wasn't Green Peace, or Antifa, or ACORN or any other 'world saving' group who 'cares.'

It was, if it happened hypothetically, a very small group of distant CIA consultants.

Rett wasn't the only one presenting this. The idea caught on (a little) and was, in fact, being repeated by louder public voices who also possess brains. The paper and its ideas went semi-viral, if you will (no pun intended), but still the sexy narrative of bioterrorism being an actual thing was too strong. It was reinforced by books, movies, and other peddlers of fiction—the news media, particularly so in covering the anthrax attacks. So while a few smart people were discussing the 'Boom Factor' idea, it never really got a grip on the masses.

But Rett's original paper wasn't targeting the masses. His was an intended audience of one. Moving one person can be much easier than moving millions, of course. Provided, that is, if one has access to the one person. A pathway.

Rett did.

That person got the message. He very much got the message. And because the man who got and read the thesis was not a lawyer but was an MBA, he understood it. The MBA-types think differently than lawyers do.

Lawyers live in a cognitive cloud. Meaning is meaningless. Fact is but rhetoric. They cognate like criminals, asking, "How can I 'get over' on someone today?" They don't concern themselves with reality because they cannot see it. The whole picture, a whole machine, is often really but a bunch of tiny details not visible to lawyers unless they can twist reality.

On the other hand, MBAs see all the details and know that the 'big picture' guy is usually a clueless hack. People with MBAs recognize that if you want to do big things, then you have to do the small things.

MBAs think logically.

The reader of the white paper was an MBA who was also the President of the United States. His mind needed all things to work logically, no loopholes. "The Boom Factor" made sense to him, though there was still a powerful public and behind-the-scenes influence which bolstered the bio-terrorism narrative.

Nevertheless, there was the right kind of bad guy who'd set up shop in a country that didn't really want that bad guy there, but the leader (dictator) of that country was trying really hard to keep a low profile since he was concerned the U.S. was in vengeance mode and wanted to make war with someone. His country didn't have anything to do with 9/11, but the public tide said, "Somebody's gonna pay the piper!"

So, the U.S. President, a Texan named Bush (or "W"), took the paper—particularly Section C—as an offer or a proposition. Then, the real Section C (hypothetically, of course) was formed (the code name 'C Section' was not chosen, but it would have been appropriate). Then, they formulated and executed a sabotage operation based on Operation Merlin (details unimportant) as a model.

It worked. Just as predicted. Just as promised. Just as written.

This greatly elevated the small team of the Section C operation along with the writer of the memo, who was also a technical/scientific advisor to the (hypothetical) operation group which hypothetically handled the hypothetical problem. Because the hypothetical team was CIA-affiliated, no one ever heard about it (contemporaneously anyway) and the hypothetical details stayed unknown. Because the bulk of the SAP (a highly sequestered designation) used contractors, the details can't even be FOIAd (FOIA, or Freedom of Information Act, requires a government agency to disclose information to the nosy taxpaying public). The hypothetical details of the hypothetical SAP operation will forever remain unknown.

Unless someone ever writes about it in a book.

But that's not going to happen.

The main point is that the very writing and disseminating of that thesis, which Rett James was compelled to do despite a lot of internalized debate, was a turning point which would affect him for the rest of his life. He just didn't know it at the time.

It wasn't a dramatic change of direction. No. It was a tiny thing. A thing he didn't really want to write, but felt he had to. It was, at the time, a course redirection that could be measured in microns. But that was enough to begin a series, a chain of causality that would later affect everything. Not just everything in his small and mostly secretive world, but literally everything. Everything and everyone. From that nearly insignificant moment on, the contours of the rest of his life were changed.

The butterfly effect.

The flap of a butterfly wing which eventually becomes a tsunami of destruction.

This is not an overstatement.

It is an observation.

The ripple did not stop with the Section C operation's completion. Not much about what followed is a joyful or happy tale. While it had those moments, they were but fleeting since the sum of all of it is tragedy, betrayal, lies, destruction, misuse of power, and subterfuge.

It is more common than anyone wishes to admit—often a villain is praised as a hero. It is also more common than anyone will allow themselves to see—a hero becomes cast as the villain.

Some might say that only the intent of the individual—his purpose—is the best judge.

Well, that's even more complicated. As an example, for a while, Rett James would say his values and morals are ossified elements of his very cellular structure, thus inalienable to himself. The fact is that there are gradations of adherence to every value, no matter how tightly one grips it. And that grip is more flexible than most would dare to admit.

Like most men, Rett James believed he was not like most men.

But also, the fact is that the ends always justify the means.

There is no precise demarcation which delineates the grey from the black and white. It is all grey. The ends justify the means.

Often people do bad things to accomplish good.

Put another way, perhaps more controversial—to accomplish the good, one must accept doing bad.

Shocking?

Not really. Not so far-fetched.

Easily relatable examples range wide.

Tell your six-year-old daughter the tooth fairy will visit her in the night.

Take an eighteen-year-old boy who would never think to take a rifle into a school to shoot school kids and teachers who is sent to some sandbox on the other side of the planet to kill a bunch of complete strangers with beards.

To the loving, but lying, parent and the well-liked patriotic boy, do the ends justify the means? Does the grey intent, as a matter of perspective only, become the metric by which we label the hero or villain?

It is a trick question.

Because the true answer is another reality that a vast majority of people—especially Americans—cannot bear to face, much less accept.

Everyone is a hero.

Everyone is a villain.

The ones who know this—who truly know it—are the ones who had to actually face it. Because you cannot learn this by hearing it or reading it. Even then, once it is learned, it is the kind of hard knowledge you try to fight against and reject. But knowledge once learned can never be unlearned.

At its core, it is an epistemological crisis.

How does one come to learn this thing our ego does not want us to even see? Nineteen hijackers and a barely circulated white paper read by a small handful of people changed the trajectory of the world.

Because of the subsequent butterfly effect, Rett James would eventually face that epistemological crisis.

It's the 'how' that is the tragedy.

NOT HERE

. . .

AFTER 9/11, THERE WAS a reorganization as the general mission changed perspective. The Agency called it a 'surge,' as if there was a sudden flood of trained and quality people instantly tasked to newly created positions of an existing playbook that had already been drawn up for a 9/11-like contingency. But that's not true. That' s not how it happened. There was no ready team on the bench, prepared to jump into the game to execute their well-practiced plays.

As much as the Agency would like to present otherwise, it was mostly people standing around saying, "So, what do we do now?!?" until someone else said, "I've got an idea."

There was a personnel surge, true, but very few could be spun up and injected into the fray immediately. In fact, mostly the surge had an initial emptying effect as those with military experience were drawn from their existing units to be re-tasked. This left holes where those people had been, in most cases, leaving a previously full team suddenly half-staffed.

Rett James's team was hit. Minus two key people, and his traditional role no longer important, the surge had not only stripped him of personnel, but of purpose.

And any sort of, well, hypothetical S&P operation against an Al-Qaeda outcast in an unwelcoming country trying to launch an aerosolization of ricin project would naturally (hopefully) be a temporary assignment. One can't exactly go to one's division chief or Agency sponsor and say, "Look, I know that Project X is over with, complete, but I'm gonna keep that open and hold on to that account for a while."

Once done, there's nothing to hold on to.

Since that wasn't going to last, obviously, Rett James had to find something else to do. Reform a new team. But to do what?

The question might have risen to near-existential level, except that Rett still had a company and a relationship to save. Anita and Rett had finally married (Rett's attempt to show how serious he was). The proposal resulted from the doldrums he felt after he'd been arrested (briefly) for—get this—burying their beloved dog on land that was a federal park. The locals, though, lacked jurisdiction for a real prosecution—there would be no charges in the end. Rett only felt good about himself when in his own element— having some mission to accomplish, with others getting out of the way until it's done.

But real life doesn't get out of the way. Real life also involves a home, a healthy relationship, people. That's all the stuff he wasn't good at in the way he thought (correctly or not) that others were.

He could handle an emerging threat to global security with ease, so why wasn't everything else so easy?

Despite the attempt, though, to make right, the couple was distressed soon after the wedding.

Rett should have known—probably did—right away. The very honeymoon day after the wedding, as Rett James was being strapped into the harness atop a very tall bungee tower, he found himself stricken by the athletic, pony-tailed blonde who was helping him tempt death by free-fall.

Maybe it was because the bungee technician was a gorgeous little gregarious blonde with that southern belle, Tennessee accent. Maybe it's because when the bungee-girl said she did these jumps all the time, his first thought was, *Anita would never even try this*. But, no matter what, the scary part was Rett's recognition that the 'old Rett' was still there, meaning he was not ready for, perhaps not even capable of, a real and committed relationship in the way that other men seem to be able to pull off so easily.

To be separated again in life, after less than a year of marriage, was a humiliating thing. That's the truth of it.

To cope with the seething failure of such a simple thing as marriage and his stagnant satellite business, he needed a distraction. He needed to do something controllable, something of his world. He needed a purpose.

Or, at least he thought he did.

Until he got one.

Once again, it was the white paper which planted that seed. Specifically, Section B, that part about assassination—something specifically forbidden for the CIA (officially) by Executive Order 12333 and multiple other statutes and regulations (so don't call it 'assassination').

But for the moment, there was an appetite to look the other way at best or to turn the entire Middle East into a parking lot at worst.

Then there was the newly introduced, semi-controversial Bush Doctrine. The Bush Doctrine said this: If you support terrorism in any way—aided, provided support, or whatever phrase you want to use—then you will be treated as a terrorist and will therefore pay the price.

It's most important to know that the Al-Qaeda network was better funded and was much more complex and structurally complicated than most countries. It was not a bunch of bearded fellows hanging about in caves. It was essentially a non-state enemy which superseded all borders. This, in some ways, made it more powerful than most countries—a non-state that transcended geography and was very sophisticated.

Some of the vital data that Rett had submitted which was mined by his people, never mind the legality of that act, brought to light a common support thread, also uncovered by the primary IC-CIA, NSA, and even the feckless FBI. A massive amount of financial support to the Al-Qaeda network was being handled (laundered) by a sophisticated bank-node web named Ktab al-dhalam.

In fact, through various vertical money transfers, which amounts to money laundering, the nineteen hijackers from 9/11 had been supported in part by Ktab al-dhalam (or Dhalam Ledger).

All nineteen of the 9/11 hijackers as well as the figurehead of the organization had direct ties to the oil-rich and U.S. allied country of Saye'ye Aylah (as it shall be called). This is where Ktab al-dhalam (Dhalam Ledger) was based, the operational funding pipeline of Al-Qaeda.

The Bush Doctrine, therefore, very much implicated Dhalam Ledger in supporting the 9/11 attacks. The money pipeline flowing into Dhalam Ledger came from all over the world (including, unfortunately, many organizations, mosques, and people even here in the U.S., as most Americans would be surprised to know). But the three primary funders of the cause, recruiting and actual operation of the 9/11 attacks which shook America to its core, were members of the Saye'ye Aylah royal family. Finding out that part was quite a shock, as he learned one day in Tennessee.

"You're kind of missing the point," Rett James told someone he'd been 'not' sent to 'not' have this hypothetical conversation with. "That section of my thesis was simply to point out that the only reliable and controllable use of chemical agents was as a tool for targeted assassination. It wasn't proposing an op!"

"Sure," replied the hypothetical man who 'wasn't there' as he sat behind the wheel of his Tahoe, parked outside of a giant flea market in Jackson, Tennessee (definitely a 'secure location'), "We get that. But you did use specific examples as to exactly how it could be done."

"Would be done," chimed in a voice from the front passenger seat, a short-framed but quiet, soft black woman. She turned her body around to the back seat as much as she could to squint at Rett James and added with a smile, "because you just said it would work. In fact, you used words like 'guaranteed.'"

The 'driver' who 'wasn't there' raised his eyebrows in the rearview mirror as he nodded to Rett James and corrected himself. "Would work then. You wrote, 'In a controlled setting, specifically a hospital, the failure rate would be 0%, under the right conditions.'"

That isn't precisely what Rett James had written, but 0.05% was certainly close enough. He decided to point out a very meaningful caveat.

"I wrote 'under the right conditions.' The 'right conditions' though and 'controlled environment' requires controlled personnel. Control of the timing. Explicit knowledge of when a specific patient would be where. In short, you'd have to have someone in on it, without them even knowing they're in on it, and manipulate everything perfectly so that your target ended up at exactly the right place, at the right time, and with the right underlying chief complaint and diagnosis. It's too much. Too many variables."

That's when Rett James, looking into that rearview mirror, saw the man's very eyes smile as he returned, "So, what if you had all that?"

Silence. Then James ventured, "Seriously? All that?"

Nothing but subtle nods from the front seat.

James shrugged, "Then there would be no trace. No way for an accurate diagnosis. No postmortem conclusion of ricin poisoning. Just—just unexplained, unexplainable, random organ failure. It might even look like natural causes or complications from something else. There would be no way for anyone to feasibly conclude assassination. Plus, the medical examiner's results could be spun, even if he had legitimate questions."

"Mmm—" the hypothetical man's lips pressed tight. "Not quite. Not a friendly medical examiner. A friendly press."

"I see," Rett James shook his head. "So, not in the U.S. then."

"Let me ask a question," the not-there man asked. "How many patients would this work on?"

Red flag!

Rett James shuddered and his skin systemically chilled. Or was it suddenly freezing in the back seat of the Tahoe? "Are you talking about some mass-casualty event?"

"No," assured the passenger seat woman. "No, no. Targeted. Controllable. Just what you wrote the President in your paper."

Clever.

First pang of regret. Maybe that too, was visible. Rett James is horrible at hiding his feelings. That's definitely something to work on.

The not-there fellow capitalized on James's emotional spillage to take the reassuring role. "You were extremely helpful in another matter, as I understand. Al-Alawki's ricin program will be an absolute bust now, right?"

Hmm. Considering that the sabotage operation from Section C was a SAP, that let Rett know how high up this guy's clearance went. But still, he wasn't on the BIGOT list for that operation.

"Yes," Rett nodded, "The instructions he has will test out, but the end product itself is a harmless decoy that won't, and it can't aerosolize either. Hypothetically, of course."

"Of course," the not-there guy replied on cue. "My question is, how many? Two? Three?"

"I—I think that all depends on the circumstances. Like I said, there are a lot of variables. What are we talking about here? A hospital setting? Do you have someone on the inside?

The right person? Is this a third-world setting? A poor hospital? Poor security? That might help."

"Definitely not a poor hospital," answered the passenger lady. "High security. Top-level technology. State of the art."

"Then you shouldn't do it," Rett replied. "Don't even think about it. It's not as easy as swapping out or forging a medical chart. All the records would be digital. Archived and even in real-time. Swapping the equipment under high security is also near-impossible. Don't do that."

"But," the not-there man gripped the wheel and looked away as a happy family exited the indoor flea market with bags loaded with American joy junk. "What kind of person would you need on the inside? Who are you saying is the right person? Because, even though you're being coy here with us—" the man's gaze returned to Rett via mirror, "I know you've already got a scenario in your head. You've already gamed this out. Or you wouldn't have put it in your paper."

Man. These guys.

Even through the closed windows of the SUV, Rett could hear the happy American flea-market Tennessean family (though people came from all over for these things) as the preteen pony-tailed girl in sun shorts munched on some fresh caramel-coated pecans while chatting with her mom about the new sparkly cat collar that Patches is just going to love. Her smaller brother trailed just behind, playing with his new keychain laser pointer.

Poor Patches.

The family passed the Tahoe, reminding Rett of who he was actually doing this for. Reminding him of what was at stake or at risk. Reminding him of what *could* be—and quite frankly, what was lost on 9/11. It was almost as if these two in the front of the SUV had somehow planned exactly for that effect, and at exactly at that moment. Impossible (was it?). But Rett did think of it and briefly, mentally accused them of it.

"Central Supply," Rett answered.

He'd worked in hospitals before. Both during clinical rotations in college, then for a year to pay back one of his scholarships. Almost all hospitals, the sophisticated ones anyway, worked the same, no matter where they were in the world.

"Central Supply?" asked the man. "Dutch—one of your instructors—told us you had medical experience. What is Central Supply?"

Dutch. Rett remembered him. One of the PM (para-military) instructors. Maybe he helped with jump school or survival school. So these people did a lot more than just read "The Boom Factor." They've been asking around.

"It's where every piece of disposable patient-use item goes and is inventoried before it is needed. Some hospitals have a more specific Surgical Supply department that acts in a similar way," Rett answered. "Just for their surgical centers."

"So you'd need an asset in Central Supply?" the hypo-thetical man asked.

"Or Surgical Supply," Rett corrected. "Depending. And you'd need a very, very skilled person to handle the... product. This time, you wouldn't be dealing with a convincing decoy. This is the real deal. To the highest yield, most concentrated, highest toxicity. Ever. Practically molecule by molecule, it would have to be perfect. Fresh, too. Proteomic structures that fragile aren't stable, they lose a lot—and quickly too.

It would almost have to be made on the spot. In country, for sure. Whatever country. You certainly can't travel with it. You'd have to develop it there. And getting the right equipment to develop that there, well, that itself is an expensive, logistical challenge. Your expert would need a lot of… stuff. No way to cut corners with it. Especially with… three, you said?"

"But it's doable?" the man nodded.

"Theoretically," Rett scrunched his face. "Who are your targets? And how do you get them to the same place at the same time? *And* make that look natural?"

"As to the targets," the woman spoke up and slid a stapled, four-page list of bank records which Rett James had seen before to the back seat. In fact, it was he who submitted hundreds of pages obtained through his own network, as obtained by Egg, through his Aussie Cicada friend. Three names were highlighted multiple times—three very large funders of Dhalam Ledger.

"I see," Rett James nodded. There wasn't much he could say. In a way, he asked for this by supplying this list in the first place. It's also not like these two were showing him something he wasn't cleared for either, since it was his damn list!

"Obviously, these three are extremely rich. Obviously providing material support. Obviously, outside of law enforcement jurisdiction or out of reach of the FBI."

"Way out of reach," scoffed the woman.

Rett continued, "Obviously, foreign. I'm going to assume Aylahi or somewhere in the Gulf. Mind if I ask, who are they?"

The woman reached into the folder for a second time, retrieving several clipped news articles printed from the internet. Still, nothing classified to any real level, just ordinary OSINT stuff.

"I don't read Gulf Arabic well," Rett noted as he held them.

"Turn them over," she motioned. "The translated version's on the back."

As Rett read, the chill returned. Funny how that happens. This strong neurological response systemically affecting the entire physical person caused entirely by nothing but non-physical thoughts and concepts inside of one's own cognition. Everyone's amygdalate expressions were different. Rett didn't become red-faced or anything. No one would ever be able to physically note his reaction, as he always appeared very calm and very controlled (no shaking, sweating, or stammering). But he could feel it. His lips dried up, almost instantly. His hands and jaw wanted to clinch. But, one thing he couldn't control very well was the sharing of his measured thoughts.

"You gotta be fucking kidding me!" Rett was not a cusser. Profanity was for lesser men. But this was unavoidable. Unsilenceable. "These people. *These* three—they're not just out of reach, they—they're untouchable! This is insane! You've literally got a prince on here!"

"There are fifty princes over there," Hypothetical Man murmured.

Rett continued. "These—these guys aren't merely extended family members. These are core members of the royal fucking family—*and* they're all very high government officials! This—" Rett shook the papers at them, "This is the shit that starts wars. World Wars! That family—that government could shut this country down. Are we prepared for that?"

"Were we prepared for 9/11?" the woman returned.

Rett shook his head, "But this would make war for real. Kinetic."

"Not if it happened to be natural causes," the man took his hands off the wheel of the parked Tahoe.

Rett continued, "This would be the most difficult, most complex, and most critical and crucial op ever! There's not a team I could think of with the experience to pull this off. The logistics, no one would get it right. You haven't developed anyone on the inside. You don't even know what or where the inside even *is* yet. This would require some real pros. Magicians, practically."

"All the experienced pros would be noticed," the man said.

"I'll bet," Rett responded. "To make all the wrong moving parts work, and I mean just right, you'd need thirty or forty of them. The best of the best. And the best chemist! I've no idea who that would be. You—to find *that* person, you really need to talk to Florence. That's who I go to."

"Florence?" asked the woman. "Florence Joseph?"

"Yes," Rett nodded. "Or, to use someone in-house, check with Florian. Mikulski."

"Funny," the woman nodded. "It's my understanding that both of them have been consulted."

"Okay," Rett nodded and sat back. "Then they'll agree that not only will your expert need a team—let's face it—from *Mission: Impossible*, but a Presidential finding for something like this. And he'll need to meet with the attorneys."

"There won't be a Presidential finding for this," she turned toward the windshield. "And I *am* the attorney. And Mr. James—"

"Yes?"

She responded, "Both Mikulski and Joseph did give a recommendation as to who best to handle this matter. Those three—untouchables, as you call them—are responsible for not only 3,000 deaths of American families, but for all of Bin Laden and Al-Qaeda attacks everywhere. I know that our recommended person will keep that in mind. It isn't just his expertise that's needed. It's also his creativity and resolve."

"Then you need to put the right people together if you want to put an end to it," Rett agreed. "I can't deny that it also sends a hell of a message, too. And I get that if you don't, then it only emboldens them further."

"I wish you'd quit saying, 'You,' Mr. James," she sighed. "The person who was recommended—was the person who wrote the paper."

"Wait—I wrote the paper!"

"And the same person," she added, "who'd previously dug up these banking records implicating Dhalam Ledger."

The chill and lip-dryness struck Rett again. "I—I don't do—I've never done anything like that before."

"No one has," she said. She reached into her folder again. What she presented him with was ordinary OSINT news stories from around the world. Pages of them. Reports on families, more than just 9/11 and victims of Al-Qaeda. Reports of Bin Laden and his surrogates bragging and claiming responsibility for the mass murder of innocents. Even a transcript of an American television reporter who, from only a few feet away, interviewed Osama Bin Laden personally, and let the man live.

Okay. She was certainly making her point.

Then it was Hypothetical Man's turn. "Rett, why are you set up at this flea market?"

Rett James was almost embarrassed to answer, but he also knew that was the point of the question. "You know I have a booth inside. I'm trying to get as many sales as I can."

The guy shook his head, "At a flea market! Does EchoStar do that? Does DirectPC? How many sales do you get from here? 20? 30?"

"No," Rett muttered, eyes narrowed.

The hypothetical man was silent a moment. "You tell us what you need. Who to develop. We'll find you what you need. We'll develop and develop quickly. There are things that you can do. That you," he motioned toward the flea market building, "actually *can* do. Do those things, Rett. Do. *Those. Things.*" Then he started up the Tahoe, "So the next 3,000 won't be lives lost, but lives saved."

YOUR OTHER FRIENDS

. . .

"HEY NIKKI," RETT SAID as he reentered his booth inside the flea market. "How we doin'?"

She appreciated when he got straight to business. "I got you three so far. Locals. Still a few hours left."

"eLocity?" Rett asked.

"No," her voice was almost a sigh. "Not computer stuff. Just TV stuff." She handed him three folders.

As Rett reviewed them, he asked, "How 'bout Brian?"

She glanced over her shoulder at the dark-haired southern boy with the swooping forehead lock, then answered, "Your boy Brian is an idiot. I don't know why you hired him. He's an id-ee-uht. Sold nothing."

"They can't all be like you, Nikki."

"Well, if they were, Rett, you'd have at least another four. He's burned everyone he talks to! He's in my way, which means he's in your way. I would have sold all four of those. As it is, his commission, even if he accidentally makes a single sale, won't even pay for his gas to get up here."

Rett nodded. Not every hire lives up to the standard Rett used to be able to expect. Maybe it's a generational thing, maybe it's a geographical subculture, but where are the driven and motivated self-starters?

"Well, try to be nice to him, Nikki. You'll need him and his truck to carry all this booth stuff back to Tupelo."

"Well, it sure isn't going in my car!" she scoffed.

"I got that," Rett raised a hand. "We'll make sure your poor Lexus still looks like its Sunday best or whatever."

He dialed his chief installer, who answered on the first ring. "Hey, Sam."

"Hey," Sam returned. "How's it goin' up there?"

"We've got four up here so far," Rett fudged the numbers with hope. Nikki frowned at him, but he ignored it.

"Four, huh? Hardly worth the trip," Sam commented. "Try to have your sales people schedule all the installs for the same day. I'll come knock 'em out."

"I did," Rett looked down at the folders, "Looks like Wednesday. You don't want to send T.J. or Lanny?"

Rett heard the sneer in Sam's voice, "No. I'll handle these myself."

Sam didn't trust T.J. or Lanny. He'd said their installs were not careful. Not 'invisible' and were substandard. In doing engineering, QC on the install teams, Sam was frequently disgusted. Rett had even been sued once because of shoddy work, which happened to be a T.J. install. Again, what happened to work ethic and pride of craftsmanship?

"Okay," Rett nodded. "Feel like bringing Brian with you to these installs?"

"No," Sam immediately countered, "Brian's an idiot."

"No, not that Brian. I mean the other one. New installer you assigned Joel to train."

"No," Sam responded. "That Brian is an idiot, too. I don't know why you hire these people. I'll take care of all the Jackson installs by myself. I can have it done in a day. I don't need someone in my way."

"Okay. Listen, Sam. I may have to take off for a week or two."

"Black belt camp?" Sam asked.

"Yeah. Something like that."

"Okay. Lemme know," Sam ended the call.

Rett turned to Nikki. "I gotta go. Try to save what's left of my marriage. Stitch us back together. Call me when you guys wrap up here."

Nikki nodded. "On again, off again, on again, off again. That's what you get for messing with little, crazy white chicks, Rett."

"Is there any other kind?"

"Are there other kinds of white girls?" Nikki clarified. "No."

"So, black girls only then?"

"Shit," Nikki suddenly poured on the stereotype. "Hell naw. We crazy, too!"

Rett packed his laptop bag. "Anita's dad is offering to buy her a house if she leaves me. This time for good. How can I compete with that?"

"Buy her a bigger house," Nikki advised.

"I can't."

"Then buy me a house."

"I can't do that either."

"Listen, Rett. What's this about you taking off for a couple of weeks?"

Rett couldn't come up with an excuse quickly enough to fool Nikki. His mental fumbling—she could see through all that.

"Oh, you got something going on, then—with your other friends."

"I don't know yet, Nikki."

"Big payday involved?"

"I don't know."

"Okay, well, just remember what you tell me—business first."

"It'll all be fine."

"Rett, you're a lousy poker player."

On his way out to his Cherokee, Rett noticed a young couple getting into their beat-up, smoking car. Parts actually held together with tape. He took that as a sign, as he thought about it. That car may not be how that couple wants this life to be. It doesn't get them any congratulatory accolades. It doesn't fill them with pride. But it gets the job done—getting them from point A to point B. Sometimes the things that need doing aren't pretty.

TERMINATION

...

Less than a week later, Rett found himself wearing a green jacket—with an escort from 'the hive'—visiting the lovely Eileen to inform her that he needed to terminate his contract.

"I've never done this before, Mrs. Reser. Is there any exit paperwork I need to sign or anything?"

"Just Eileen, hun. That depends on why you're quitting. Is it a permanent thing, orrrr?"

She had been down this road before. She knew what corners could be cut. Exits from the CIA, the permanent ones, no matter if a blue-badger or an SGE, or even a standard green-badged IC (employee of a contracted company) are not an instant process. For some, it takes months. Rett was an SGE. Not hard to let go of, but there's still a process.

"Well, I've got to handle a different matter. TDY. But there'd be a conflict of interest, you see. So, I really don't know when or if I'd be back.

"Okay, hun. Then let me print out a couple things. Fill them out here in Headquarters and get them to your branch chief. He'll get them back to me."

Rett wanted to comply with her. After all, she's a redhead

and super charming, with all the power and grace of a woman three decades his senior, but—"I don't have access to him today. Can I give all this to my agency sponsor? What about someone from legal? I have to visit an attorney while I'm here."

"Legal will work just fine, hun. And good luck."

"Thank you, Mrs. Re—uh—Eileen."

"You're welcome, Rett." She glanced down at Rett's freshly printed badge.

Rett's later meeting was merely a statement saying that he was in, followed by a scheduling off-site for later that day, since all felt it could not be officially held or planned inside that building, nor any space there shared with a hall-walker who has no official account.

Later that afternoon, Rett outlined to a very small group exactly who, what, how, and when—down to every tiny detail—to make it all happen according to his primary, an alternative, and even a contingency plan.

"I'm still working out an emergency plan," he informed the incredibly high-level people at the secure off-site location (minus the attorney, whose job was to not know any details).

"There's an important caveat," the highest ranked in the room growled.

"What's that sir?" Rett asked.

"Do not make contact at all with any C/O in that country. And if you have any contact at all with any U.S. diplomat, it will be entirely as your cover, for agricultural business purposes only. No backdoor communications with Agency, even if you have trouble. Especially if you have trouble, any trouble of any kind. This includes even the COS."

"Really, sir?"

"Yes, really. The COS in that capital city isn't going to know and will not even be informed of a damn thing."

"Yes, sir. Okay."

Wow. Nothing could be further off the books than this. It is entirely understandable why.

The highest-ranking man added, "So you presented that you could get in, neutralize their ability to fund Dhalam Ledger, then get out without making even a splash. Everything looks solid. Obviously we can't run this past too many people. Who would you like—or trust— to double check everything?"

"Whoever you wish, sir. Whoever you trust. The way I see it, as long as I get everything I ask for and things go as planned, in and out, both should be a cake walk. Invisible. No one will notice."

"Okay then, son. Everything you asked for, you will have. As soon as we have it all in place, we'll let you know. Meanwhile, we'll help you get your team together. Even if we have to pull these people away from whatever, wherever they're doing. We'll make this work."

"Yes, sir."

THE ANTHILL

• • •

Maybe it is because Rett James had always felt (right or wrong) as if his previous contributions really didn't amount to much of anything. Maybe it's because he knew others were contributing in ways that were important. Or, maybe it is because he detested—and so never tried—playing the political kiss-up game with the cliquish IC (Intelligence Community) D.C. 'in crowd' whom he thought were too analyst-centric. It might even have been because most in the IC 'society' held master's degrees and PhDs from their Ivy League recruitment-qualifying political science, intelligence studies, or strategic studies programs (all of which didn't exist just a decade prior) that he felt under-qualified, therefore easily ignored.

It is certainly true that the administrative hierarchy promotes from within the family, but in that family—both the Beltway Bandits and those directly of the DO (Directorate of Operations)—the field workers seemed to be distant cousins. Those in the field were specialists often by education, but generalists by practice—unlike the classroom-instructed CAPS coterie who lived within a quick drive from Langley and lunched together, drank together, and recreated together.

The DI analysts, who swarmed the ant mound of Headquarters all day, cast judgments (often wrong) and made decisions (often wrong) about the quality of what intel a C/O (case officer in the DO) had sent, or considered (often wrong) what some field-based officer should do (who is often thousands of miles away), or often debated a report's placement of a comma or redundancy. The DO people stayed as insular as possible, knowing that it was them, the DO, that really did all the work—even without a PhD.

So it was easy for the risk-taking war horses of the DO to have little regard for the soft, self-congratulating analysts of the DI (Directorate of Intelligence). And little care if the pedigreed of 'the DI lefties' knew how they were thought of by the DO. A lot of the DO lived and breathed—and even worked (regular, or 'civie' jobs)—amongst the fabric of real America. They lived in the cornfields of flyover country, the pines of the deep south, the rocky shores of the northern coasts, and the deserts of the southwest. They thought differently than those in the Beltway because they lived differently. Or maybe it was the other way around—maybe CIA field officers tend to live differently because they think differently, quietly fitting their TDY assignments into their lives, intermixed with their 'civie' life. It may be a lot harder, emotionally, psychologically, and even physically, to live such a double life, something those living a commute away from Langley who scanned through security turnstiles every day didn't have to worry about. That's why the DI job expectancy is much longer and the churn much lower. Still, those of the DO generally don't fit so well. And they know to use Headquarters as a resource for getting their next project approved or done—not how to use it as a country club.

Rett's propensity for insularity was likely based on all that, given some introspection (even 20 years too late), so it was quite a shock to think that now, suddenly he was considered critical for a unique task of this magnitude.

He never thought his periodic reporting on payload telemetry for foreign satellites was ever useful to anyone. Busy work. All he was doing had been filling a (low) paid position just so that some box somewhere could be checked. Or signal-sniffing in a place of no consequence.

This feeling of low worth was becoming common at the moment in the understaffed DO that had not trained the sudden post-9/11 recruits up to speed yet.

Here's why: The 9/11 effect spurred DO officers to patriotic fervors to do something meaningful to protect their beloved country, but when not much actually changed (unless you were one of those surged to support the DOD or a paramilitary mission) and once DO officers began saying, "What am I doing?"—feeling even less consequential than before—they started leaving the Agency. Particularly as their own assessments from the field (especially regarding Iraq) blatantly contradicted the general and public sentiment which was seemingly being controlled by the DOD wing of that administration.

What Rett should have done was step back from himself for a moment, including his own drive and hyper-motivation propensities, and evaluate in a dispassionate, logical manner. Had he done so, he might have asked the popular (but unvoiced) question of the day for CIA officers in the field—"Am I being used? Am I but an expendable toy for those safe anthill dwellers, sent out to do what they can't, based on a guess? Am I actually critical, or an expendable pawn?"

He should have asked these questions.

He didn't.

LIVING IN THE '80S

• • •

ONE OF THE COGNITIVE problems with logic-based thinkers like Rett is they skip right past asking the question "Should I do X?" and instead jump to "*How* do I do X?"

This easily leads to moral dilemmas in that the primary qualifying question should be whether or not to do something in the first place.

This absence of moral caution is frequently confused with extreme over-confidence or outright arrogance. This is because it presumes that the moral debate has been settled.

For example, when one is already considering a *How do I… ?*, then the assumption is that all of the factors which are part of the *Should I do… ?* have already been decided in favor of the action—such as considerations of effect on other people and so on—thus arrogantly turning a *How do I… ?* into the appearance of a *How can I get away with… ?*.

The question *How can I get through this yellow light?* presumes that the *Should I… ?* question is decided and thus looks like an arrogant entitlement to the streets. It looks like: *How can I get away with having no caution here?*

Here's a more powerful example: *That insanely delicious*

redhead who could be with any man on the planet is really into me. So how can I coordinate an affair with her, since I am incapable of saying no to that?

Skipping to the 'how' part completely waives any and all of the factors of the *Should I... ?* equation. The *Should I... ?* equation would demand some further contemplation: *Is she really into me, or really just into herself? Given my weakness—the inability to say no—is that really something which should be fed? Most importantly, since this woman is not my wife (or fiancé/girlfriend, whatever) isn't this an extreme moral hazard?*

Short-circuiting the *Should I... ?* question is nearly always a very bad idea. For some, like Rett, it isn't because of a choice made out of arrogance ("My instant feelings are more important") nor a habit of super-optimism ("such-and-such will never know—I am so good at what I do"). With people like Rett, the *should* was not willingly bypassed; it was never even a possibility for consideration. This is because their cognition is wired so as to be so interested, so focused, so intent on knowing the minutiae and processes and problem-solving that they go right to critical analysis and strategic planning, leaving out the human elements. This includes the human questions. An extreme example of that cognition might be a chemical engineer who is autistic, or even an autistic mathematician.

So that is the place where Rett's mind was taken (from that day forward at least), including on his way to and at MITRE as he met with his friend later that day.

"Tad, look at this," Rett laid out several pages of sketching, frequency charts, details and notes. "Tell me if this is something that can work?"

Tad Henninger pored over Rett's mess of a design, but clearly got the gist right away. "*Can* work, or *will* work, Rett?"

If it had been a lesser brain posing the question, Rett might have taken it personally. "What's wrong with it?"

"What exactly are you trying to do? Cook a turkey from across the street?"

Rett smiled and shook his head, almost snickering, "Something like that, yeah. I imagine you can see what's up here. I don't wanna go into it. Won't."

Tad nodded once. "I was informed, I'm not gonna say by who—but it was Florian—to help you with anything you want. But what you've got here, it looks like you don't need me for anything. You've practically built this by yourself—and with off-the-shelf stuff."

"That's one place where I need help building it. I don't know what else is out there that's *not* off-the-shelf. I don't know if there's new tech that'll help me get there. Plus, I don't know what software I'll need to coordinate the input variables. That'll help me build it, too."

"Okay, Rett. That's two. What else do you need from us? To help you build it?"

"Umm—well—that would be the 'building it' part too."

Tad laughed. "You open to improvements? Efficiencies?"

"Of course, Tad. I'm open to everything. I have very little time to get it done."

"How much time?"

Rett scrunched his face. "Well—that's the other thing—"

"Uh-oh."

"Four days."

Tad laughed again. "No. Seriously, man."

Rett chuckled. "Yeah. You're right. That's crazy. Four days."

"You *are* serious."

"Very."

Tad looked at the drawings and specs. "Okay, then. These three triangulating frequencies don't need to be precisely the same."

"I was thinking of generating wave interference."

"But that could work both ways, Rett. Interference can enhance waveform patterns. But, it can also cancel things out, too. Didn't you consider the de Broglie formula, at least?"

"Uh, sorry. I should have. I didn't do the math. Plus, in my design here, I wasn't sure I could obtain what I needed for many microwave generators of more than one frequency."

"Well, next time, do the math."

"Yes, sir."

"I mean, did you just draw this shit up yesterday? Or on the way over here? This shit is amateur, man. When did you think this up?"

"Long story."

"I'm on your time. Let's hear it."

"Okay. When I was 17, I started a decade-long career in radio broadcasting."

"Okay—"

"One of my friends there was an engineer. The station I was working, Q101, had a studio in one place, but the transmitter and tower was miles away on top of a massive hill overlooking the entire city. The studio feed was microwaved into that transmitter."

"I'm quite aware of how microwave transmitters work, Rett. But thank you soooo much for the tutorial. Let me guess, you guys actually did try to cook a turkey?"

"No. But, in winter, I did notice some variances and aberrant icing effects. Even on the reflect-back."

"I see. That's not proper syntax, but I understand where you're going."

"So, essentially, Tad, I've been thinking about concentrating these effects since 1988 or so."

"Hm. And this was the best you could do?"

Rett's answer was a blank stare.

"Listen, Rett. You think you've innovated something here. But you haven't. Hell, microwave cannons already exist. DARPA tested one a decade ago the size of a grenade launcher. Instant effects. Temporary, but they can linger, even after the bombardment ceases for a while. I don't know if they ever tested triangulated effects on a target, but if that's what you want, then the existing microwave cannons are a better place to start for you because—get this—they're tunable."

"Really?"

"Yeah, really. You should keep up with this stuff, Rett."

"So you're actually jumping my ass for coming up with an amazing invention."

"That's already been invented."

"—but not knowing that. Jumping my ass for not knowing something existed that is so uber-secret that no one's supposed to know it exists. Am I getting that right?"

"A week," Tad offered. "Using DARPA designs, I could probably get a semi-concealable version of this done in seven days."

"Four. Four days."

Tad's eyes narrowed. "Maybe they still have a few. Maybe we could just get theirs and customize three of them. You'd still need software to coordinate the signals and three separate IR rangefinders to maximize the apertures for optimal focus. And some sort of an interface between all the equipment and your controlling unit, say a laptop. Soo… six days."

"I've got a guy who can build the interface. I'm assuming each unit will have two outputs and one input? Four days. This isn't a negotiation."

"Who's your guy?"

"A kid back home. Meridian, actually. High school dropout whiz kid named Egg that I've used for builds before."

"Egg?"

"Nickname," Rett waved. "I imagine each unit can be serial cabled."

Tad snorted. "There you go, not thinking again. You gonna run serial cables all over the streets of whatever probably hostile place you're going? Stop. You still living in the '80s?"

"It was a good time for me."

"No, man. We'll give each unit independent power and wirelessly network the data of each to 802.11g or VHF. There are your data streams. This way your targeters need not be anywhere near each other, as long as they have line of sight to your target. Tell him that."

Rett felt silly. "Okay."

"Five days," Tad began folding the useless design.

"Four days, Tad. That's all I've got."

"Okay, man. But you owe me big after this one, Rett."

"You'll have to wait in line then, Mr. Henninger. Right now, I seem to owe everyone else."

SPARK

...

"A TINY SPARK CAN change the world." And it does every day.

That is an age-old adage most people are familiar with in the sociological sense. Generally when someone says such a thing, it is in some sort of motivational speech designed to empower someone in a positive way (though obliviously negative ways also apply). So it's an overused, ubiquitous cliche, really, which has lost its power in that sense.

"Hey you. Get off your butt and do one tiny good deed for the day. Be the change you want to see and it'll catch fire around the world. Blah blah blah."

Nonsense. All of it.

The sentiment is fine. And, it is a good (although completely obvious) way to live and live with integrity. However, quite frankly, the reality is that the inaugurating event of a butterfly effect has zero bearing on a final outcome further down the causal stream of it. A positive or good deed today can just as easily lead to a bad—even harmful—outcome later. The likely event is no outcome or effect at all, particularly so in sociological matters.

Why? It's not just a sample size.

It's because no one really cares anymore. Especially about the good deeds. Do one good deed and the best response one could expect might be a verbalized appreciation.

The bad deeds, however—even an aberrant, isolated event and of no actual societal impact—can be as societally effective (to no end of exaggeration) as an extinction-level event. A single bad deed can move people not merely to voice an opinion but to act as an army. A single event—a single thoughtless, seemingly insignificant moment or deed— if bad, can (and often does) cause riots, catastrophic political upheavals, and even war.

So, from a sociological point-of-view, the intended meaning behind the phrase has, well, lost its meaning.

"A tiny spark can change the world."

Here, though, is how that phrase is very true, and in a novel way, never discussed anywhere (though it is so interesting that it's worthy of a lifetime of contemplation). And it is a literal example.

Neurochemically, a thought has immense power. It is the most powerful thing in the human world. This is not psychobabble 'feel good' fluff to say that a thought becomes reality. Well, actually it is or *can be*, depending on context, but it's much more than that, because it is real.

This is to say, not some mere discussion of perception— like considering how one thinks of the world, so it is, or thinking one can change one's reality by changing one's thoughts. That's pseudo-scientific psychobabble. It's meaningless tripe peddled by insecure psychologists, therapists, or counselors—none of whom, by the way, are actual medical doctors—sharing the practiced skill of making a client feel better temporarily while convincing them something real and scientific was done.

No.

Aside and despite the psychobabble of it, there is a way in which it is true that a single thought, a single notion which is but a neurological reaction inside of a single person's head, actually becomes externalized as reality.

Here's what that means.

Your tiny electrochemical spark between neurons is your reality, yes. But also, your tiny electrochemical spark between neurons is everyone else's reality.

That which is but a tiny spark between two neurons inside of our head, that which is entirely internal, that which we think— that becomes external, can become influence, can literally change the entire world.

Your neurochemical electrical patterns are your thoughts, notions, and potential actions that, when expressed (as written, spoken, or acted), become injected into, thus affect, the actual reality around you.

So that tiny neuronic nanospark is much more important than anyone thinks. In fact, that spark *IS* thinking, itself!

A notion in someone's head, internal, becomes everyone else's reality. That is, in fact, how humanity advanced. A notion which came from some other person's spark, becomes not only accepted, but adopted and perpetuated.

Just like philosophical words on a page. They are someone else's notions, someone else's spark, which then becomes a new spark between the neurons of a reader, now contemplating (sparking) what was just read or previously written and questioning meaning and why it was written in the first place.

The white paper ("The Boom Factor") had begun as merely a spark amongst the trillions of sparks in Rett James's head. A neurochemical waveform pattern that he couldn't shut off for days until he externalized it—expressing it onto paper. Once externalized (then properly disseminated) he found he could somewhat let go of it, making room for trillions of other sparks.

Funny how that works. Often, the only means of peace from a spark pattern which haunts you is to express it, such as writing it down.

And yet, in finding that peace—because that cognition is no longer internal, now part of reality—*that* is when the real trouble can start.

Because now that Rett's once insular sparks become part of the reality for others, those others can then latch onto the expressed notion and make something manifest of it, or force him to.

Had Rett kept his spark—his notions—to himself, he wouldn't be dealing with it right now.

Nor would anyone else.

The butterfly effect, as progressed downstream, have no other result than world-changing. That's another fascinating thing about it. Some people have sparks which nearly always result in global impact or massive change. It is fascinating that, ontologically, dramatic changes are not generally the result of nations or societies or populations. Dramatic changes are caused by individuals. Groups don't spark history, individuals do.

Equally as fascinating is that, although history is made by sudden, unanticipated—even accidental—individual acts, it is also sometimes the same individuals who spark change, spark history multiple times. It is as if some people's sparks are more contagious than others.

If those highly contagious sparkers had kept that spark to themselves, then often the world would be a calmer place.

But, once externalized—particularly with the contagious sparkers—something is going to happen. There will be effects.

Sometimes that is bad (the Holocaust, 9/11, this operation, etc..), but sometimes it is good. Sometimes it is bad when *not* externalized. Imagine being absolutely in love with someone but never telling her. The result of not expressing that notion will likely be an absolute denial of a future with her. Not only have you cheated yourself out of that possibly beautiful future, but she has been cheated from it, too.

Yet, Rett could also realistically tell himself that expressing the very same notion, even when unsure of his own notion himself further down the line of the causal chain, would be a negative. One thing he can remind himself of from experience is that such externalization of notions (expressing) can be exactly what someone else is looking for. And, as previously stated, latched onto—not allowing him any escape from it, being captured by and into his own notion. Thus causing him to regret expressing it.

Sometimes he knew this. He's damned if he does express it and damned if he doesn't.

The thing about life is that no matter how well one plans things out, you never really know what the end result will be (planning helps, but doesn't guarantee).

Operationally, this is why those in the DO recognize that even the best planning, with thorough attention to detail and extensive practice, is not much more than what those in the DI experience in predicting outcomes.

Which is why the DI analysts refuse to do it. The most anyone can get a CIA analyst to commit to is saying, "High level of confidence that—" As much as this frustrates other people dealing with the squishy analysts of the DI ("Well, is Ellen Johnson-Sirleaf going to win the Liberian election on her own or not? Just give me a straight answer!"), operators within the DO have had to adopt a similar phobia of absolute commitment to expressing any kind of guarantee. If it *can* go wrong, it *will* go wrong.

Rett believed strongly in over-preparedness. In fact, he taught his people a creed of "Leave no doubt!" which requires extensive planning, tactical and creative trouble-shooting, and copious, diligent practice. But his main superpower was his ability to anticipate really big and even really small problems at all times. Always expect problems everywhere.

Some people call that anxiety.

Of course, some people even call it paranoia.

But, Rett called it a potentially justifiable prognostication and a tactical awareness of a need for sudden reevaluation. Prudence. In fact, the only time Rett expected to be surprised is if things actually went exactly according to plan. Or better. And how often does that happen?

Especially when there are people involved. One thing he could say about people: It is only a matter of time until they let you down.

That 'people' includes the self.

So, no matter how sideways this thing goes, there was plenty of blame he could preserve for himself.

It was *his* spark.

He could have kept it to himself.

And obviously, he can't do that very well.

Obviously.

REDUNDANT NETWORK

...

ONE OF THE PROBLEMS in creating a network of assets (be they agents for intelligence-gathering or an operational asset) is that the CIA's standard process, predevelopment, is often slow, clunky, and even arbitrary with its approvals. In the field, Headquarters likes to thoroughly vet and approve anyone doing anything. Some time back, a few DCIs prior to George Tenet, a seventh-floor edict came down preventing recruitment, development, and, to a degree, mere association with 'unsavory' types.

This was a huge monkey-wrench which had an instant negative effect on the ability of CIA-DO officers to do their job. Telling those in the DO, "Don't do business with criminal types or bad people" is obviously going to cripple the DO. And so it did.

If we are going to bribe a recruited foreign lawmaker to vote for a U.S. interest, then by definition, we are doing business with a dirty politician. The whole point of the CIA is that we often have to get in the mud and muck with 'unsavory types' in order to get things done. The recruited asset who is going to betray his country by giving a CIA handler his country's national secrets is not going to be a choir boy.

Association with those 'non-choir boys' is the entire point. It was a flawed edict which made no sense. But, of course, the analyst-centric seventh floor of the CIA did not understand that. Of course the analysts, safely tucked away in Langley—who only associate with each other and suburban Virginians—have the luxury of thinking and seeing through their G-rated, rose-colored lenses. The DI folks (analysts) sipping from their Agency Starbucks don't have to do the job of core collectors (they just bitch about the work product) and other operatives of the DO who are scattered around the world in very dark places, most of which don't share the values of the suburbanite Virginians of the DI.

All of this is to say that the CIA had already previously told Rett to no longer associate with certain people who were considered criminals (or close to it) or had problematic associations of their own.

Now, the usual approval process would have taken too long for the current project. That was just fine for Rett James, who would have utilized the greater latitude and autonomy contractors typically have anyway. But in this case—so completely clandestine that it didn't exist—Headquarters would have no real say anyway. Besides, Rett wouldn't have cared.

It was Rett's own standard which he followed here, which was: Even though the CIA will coordinate (unofficially, but that itself is official—it's complicated) to get Rett every *what* and every *who* he needed, Rett will still set up his own redundant network just the same. Of his own people. Sometimes of assets the CIA had officially forbidden and sometimes of those never even reported or that the Agency didn't even know about. (Reporting can be fudged later—something that is a very serious disciplinary matter.) But, the job gets done.

Isn't that what matters?

So, even as the (un)official team was coming together, Rett was coordinating behind the scenes to task an internationally 'wanted' hacker of a labeled criminal enterprise to penetrate the computerized medical records systems of a particular hospital. Access gained now will be access used very soon.

"Find or make a door that we'll need to open and use soon."

Meanwhile, he informed the five 'official' members of his assemblage.

"Your primary job will be to get all three targets to the hospital." Then he showed them the three pulsed microwave cannons (now smaller than the DARPA design) and how to use them so they could practice.

And so they did. In fact, twice Rett had to caution and stop them from practicing on each other (a few of them were ex-military and special forces guys have a twisted sense of humor).

But, Rett himself could only practice his part in his head as his unique delivery design required serious innovation. Challenge met and solved. What he designed was a micro-encapsulation of what would need to be nano-sized particles, hardly larger than the ricin-chain molecule itself (which is a rather large nitrogen-based molecule) so as to be as unnoticeable as dust in the air. The encapsulating membrane was a hydrophobic lipid (redundant) which would break down under higher pressures of concentrated oxygen, releasing the encapsulated 'dust.' Moreover, the spheres had to be small enough to fit through the lumen of an 18-gauge needle. That needle would never come anywhere near a single target.

Ideally, not a single member of Rett's team would come anywhere near the targets.

However, the innovative design of the product itself could only be practiced in the abstract. Rett did not own any of the sophisticated laboratory equipment which would be needed. No rocker, no centrifuge, no aerosolizer, no tubes, no pipette, no epitaxy chamber—nothing. Rett did not own a microscope (not since childhood) or even a pair of tweezers. Nothing that would raise a red flag. All that stuff would be found in-country when he arrived, and only then could he develop his signature molecular-chained structure (which would actually be his second). Once again, he will have been the very first to develop an original product, but this time it wouldn't be the testable decoy of his previous strain. Neither is it something you really want to put your name on a patent for. This one actually would violate a war crimes treaty (the previous one couldn't—legally anyway).

But there will be no practice. He will have to hope and assume that he has it all correct in his head (and, as usual, scratched out on paper).

He will, in essence, get only one shot at it.

By mid-July, they'd familiarized themselves with their covers (three of them, Rett included, were fertilizer purchasing agents looking to commission manufacturing) and their tasks, studied their targets and established their network, as well as committed to memory (almost) all the relevant exit scenarios, safe-houses, and just about all the logistics from primary to emergency.

Nearing the end of the month, it was time. Time for the most daring CIA operation since Rolando Cubela (1965).

20%

• • •

How did Rett James end up at the bottom of an elevator shaft? is not the real question. That part was known—at least by him—and was immaterial anyway since it was too late to address the *how*.

The questions in Rett's mind were different. In fact, it was a series of *What if?* questions that gripped his attention. Reviewing causal chains of life choices from as far back as decades ago and 10,000 miles away was probably a coping mechanism so as to not recognize or deal with dying.

Or, more accurately, the cessation of living.

Rett James refused to die here.

This late July, in a distant foreign city, in a hospital, in an elevator shaft. The bottom of it. Surrounded by fragile, ancient fluff-dust which resembled grey cotton candy with little more consistency than smoke.

No. He couldn't let himself die here.

He had other things to do.

He wasn't finished yet.

Not finished with this mission. Not finished with his plans. Not finished with life.

As if refusing death could prevent it.

It doesn't.

He didn't yet know, though, that he was soon to be dead. For four months or so.

It's complicated.

Other men his age (now 31) didn't have to deal with these kinds of things. Those guys were out on the town, dancing with some smiling 26-year-old blonde. Seeing a movie with their young kids. Going to church choir practice with grandma. Recording a favorite sitcom. Maybe other guys Rett's age were just driving down the perfect road with a happy dog in the passenger seat, his face sticking out the window, ears and tongue flapping in the wind.

Other guys Rett's age weren't stuck at the bottom of an elevator shaft in a hostile country.

Other guys got to have a life.

And then they got to keep it.

Other guys Rett's age could line up all their life choices in front of them like ice cream flavors for comparison. They got to make sound and simultaneous evaluations in order to select just the right one. Then they got to enjoy it.

One thing to remember about being stuck (or hiding) at the bottom of an elevator shaft in order to avoid being shot—there follows a lot of introspection of a life which could soon end.

Cessation of breathing.

That would leave so many things unfinished, undone, and unresolved.

This is not the best time to go.

It is often said that at or near the end of life, as old remorse begins to surface, the bulk of our regrets are not about things which were done but things which should have been done.

"I should have—"

Doing (or not) those 'should haves' is much easier to evaluate in retrospect, without the urgent prescience of the emotionally burdening warnings (usually fear) of some catastrophic future or another.

Rett James was a man of misplaced fears.

He was not afraid of anything physically. Nor are most men until they hit age 35, probably (it is a miracle any man ever reaches 30). Physically, he would directly take on and challenge any person, provocation, task, or dare, often creating or inventing new ones just 'to do.' Adrenaline is the primary fuel of youth.

Many people could look at that characteristic and proclaim, "How brave he is!"

Older (wiser) people would view the same but respond, "How stupid!"

Ask a life insurance agent if his snake handler client is brave or foolish. If the professional stuntman is fearless or daft. If the stunt pilot is ballsy or reckless. There is a reason there can be no answer to those questions: There is no such client. None of these people can even get life insurance. They cannot qualify for the sensible things in life. Adrenaline, like fire, drinks the same oxygen as sensibility, making coexistence unlikely—if not impossible.

Rett James's fears were of a different sort. His fears were of an unstable future. Lack of preparation now would surely lead to a future failure. Indulgence now means less resources later. Therefore, a warped concept of a blurred creed caused a fear of current happiness, of current indulgence. As if happiness is a finite resource that if it were tapped into and drank from now, there will be drought later. Rett held a secret guilt against enjoying the moment. As if it felt wrong to be happy in the now. Being happy now meant not being frugal with that limited resource, cheating the future. It was wrong to indulge now. Selfish. It cheats the future self. So, it follows then that being unhappy was a sign of being a responsible adult.

So Rett never pursued happiness. Only the thing which made him unhappy (the responsible thing—obviously). And that is, in part, why his leadership was trusted—because he's such a serious person with all his ducks in a row.

But at the end of life, or whenever facing that, one doesn't reflect and celebrate themselves for being such a serious person. One doesn't comfort himself by saying, "I was a good leader." One never has as his last thought that he was so happy to have been detail-oriented.

Those are not a dying man's comforts. But because Rett James had lived his life in fear, only glancing at indulgences and happiness through a living lens of envy and guilt, he never took the opportunity to do a quality evaluation in a simultaneous way.

He never sampled the ice cream flavors in front of him before making the purchasing decision.

Instead, he was a sequential evaluator in life. This leads to problems. Big ones. It doesn't, for example, allow proper means to answer basic questions like "Who do I marry?"

Sequential evaluation and analysis does not allow for direct or actual comparison. That is, *not* seeing all the choices at the point of evaluation leads to poor choice-making. Poor evaluating. Luck, or none.

His proclivity (born of fear) to delay gratification has cheated him of life's indulgent moments. We are taught that delaying gratification is the responsible thing. The reality is that those two concepts (gratification and responsibility) are completely unrelated to each other, linked solely by vestigial remains of borrowed and indoctrinated moral codes. The very same fear of a diminished future (which requires delaying gratification) more often comes at a cost. Quality of life—life in the existing moment—is an un-ignorable component of happiness. A healthy enjoyment of the moment is what true wisdom seeks.

This is why he was seldom in control of his romantic relationships. As long as he let her (whichever her) make the decisions and guide the direction of things, as long as she (whichever she) led the dance, then he could be sure that he wasn't to blame for the missteps.

That fear guaranteed that others made the relationship choices; all he had to do was follow. Though obviously that often led to serious conflict when following the dance of multiple dance partners at the same time. Avoiding decisions out of fear is not only cowardly, it is undisciplined. And to Rett, lack of discipline was abhorrent.

Meaning the hyper-disciplined Rett James considered his fear-induced poor decision-making self-abhorrent and everything that he, himself, wouldn't tolerate. Abrogating a sense of personal agency to an external influence is the exact opposite of practicing individual cognition. And individual cognition was supposedly the very essence of an Objectivist like Rett. Thus, turning over all relationship choices and putting someone else in the driver's seat only ensured Rett was always a passenger.

So, even the marriage question was never even a valid consideration for him. Evaluation of that choice, and all the others of a relationship which precede that, was not up to him—the passive passenger, simply along for the ride, lest he be criticized for making a misstep.

But the others his age—that is to say, those not afraid or ashamed of life's indulgences—recognize that missteps are an important part of their experience. Most people give themselves a tolerable allowance of missteps. They call that 'being human' or some such thing.

For whatever reason, that 'being human' was never allow-able to Rett. Even as a child, he rejected it (just as he rejected childhood, itself—supposedly an experience others enjoyed).

Not taking the lead in the dance of love—all that he did not do by abrogating his decision-making—ranked high in his regrets.

Those regrets were now amplified inside this elevator shaft, punctuated each time the hospital's service elevator car squeaked its way to the basement floor or merely sat there (as it often did) causing Rett to duck or crook his head sideways at an unnatural angle if he wanted to sit upright. He quickly found it best not to try. After less than the first 22 hours on the shaft floor, which was about 6:00 p.m. on the second day of his hideaway, he'd learned to simply lay down and stay down until the service elevator car was called to any higher floor, most commonly the ground floor.

It was about a day into it and onto the second calendar

day, that he tried to sweep the decades of accumulated cotton candy-ish dust to a corner. It was brittle and dry, but sticky when he did so, throwing up a smothering cloud that, without any ventilation, lingered, causing him to taste it and worse. He coughed, sneezed, and sniffled for at least an hour. This was extremely dangerous, since, if the car was low enough, he could have been easily heard by an elevator passenger or the men with guns who were searching.

Searching for him.

Men who carried guns, particularly those who would be assigned to hunt someone, were good with them. Well trained.

Rett James wasn't armed with a gun.

Spy movies and spy books usually do a massive disservice to the truth of the operational integrity of the real world. Neither the handlers (the spy-recruiters interested in obtaining intel) nor the specialized operators (including support) made it a habit to run around with a gun. In fact, carrying one at all is a very bad idea. Firing it definitely meant something went very wrong. If a gun is involved at all, then there was a problem, and likely will be another. Truth be told, it is good to not need to rely on the very limited training CIA recruits receive. While they did spend plenty of time at the range, the only weapons required to qualify on—despite the training on nearly everything—was the heavy Browning 9mm, and later, the Glock 9mm (the standard-issue pistols). Rett found that his favorite was actually a Kel-Tek .32 cal, silenced, since it tended to stay on target as underpowered and front-heavy as it was when suppressed. But that was safely at home, on the other side of the planet, in its blue zipper case in Mississippi—which would do him no good here.

Not that it would anyway. While Rett may be a better shot than the average person, he was certainly not an expert and was therefore very far from the typical Spy-Fi myth of books, movies, and television.

While harrowing moments do happen in the course of operations, shootouts are extremely rare and to be avoided—also unlike the myth provided by fiction writers.

A gunfight in this hospital, against the armed and trained men who were searching for him, would be a terrible idea. First, the chance of winning is absolutely zero (also unlike books and films). Not only are the hunters better trained and with larger and more accurate weapons, there is an infinite number of reinforcements just a radio call away. Plus, there's a chance they are wearing protective vests, whereas Rett James was wearing the hospital scrubs common of a lab technician, orderly, or Central Supply.

Secondly and most importantly, engaging in a gun fight obviously reveals that Rett is actually there. And at the moment, the hunters are operating on a notion, a natural extension of their normal security-protective detail duties for the very high-level protectees under their charge. They 'felt' that Rett was there—must be there, somewhere—an intuition that Rett completely failed to account for during operational planning.

It's an unexplainable phenomenon—that intuition. And it is nearly always correct, but almost always also unexplainable, even if one was to directly question the professionals who do that work. In the United States, the equivalent protective professionals who exemplify this would be USSS (United States Secret Service), DSS (State Department's Diplomatic Security Service) or GRS (CIA's Global Response Staff). If one was to question them as to how anyone knew something was going to happen, they might provide sketchy details, but the real answer is almost always, "I don't know—I just—felt it. Something just felt wrong." And that's just not the kind of answer they could write in the AAR.

Those types of protective professionals have keener instincts than the rest of humanity, and may well be why they do what they do, simply because of that superpower intuition. Their 'Spidey-sense' is hardly ever wrong.

This is yet another way Rett James was seriously outmatched.

The protectors-turned-hunters just knew he was there, somewhere.

He just had to be.

It couldn't possibly be coincidence that three high-level officials who were all core members of the royal family ended up dead and at the same exact hospital, practically all at the same time.

The hunters were right.

Rett James knew his only choice (which means *not* a choice) was to make their intuition a lie. All of them. Every one of them had to come to the conclusion that their never-wrong professional instincts were completely wrong.

So this was a matter of patience, endurance, determination, and a lot of fear. He must stay secluded in this elevator shaft until the professionals—who were convinced he was there—stopped searching.

Either he had to make *them* wrong or be wrong himself.

Dead wrong.

He also had to account for their manner of thinking, which might well be that there's more than one manner of searching. He considered that they would begin with a tentative what-if type of search, which would contagiously become a perpetuated active search. This active-search phase may even include sensor technology, reviewing all camera footage (and, unlike movies, hospital cameras do not cover every square inch of every floor, room, office, or suite), strict scrutiny of every worker, volunteer, patient, and family member, and even more draconian tactics if they felt it justified.

In fact, twice since his hideout began, an elevator door on higher floors had been forced open and flashlight beams scanned this service elevator's shaft. The beams were stilted and clumsy. Rett suspected this was because of the logistical problem that the flashlight searcher likely was not the same person who was holding the sliding doors apart. Also, the flashlight searcher would not feel comfortable leaning too far over to peer deep into the chasm. This made it easy and logical for Rett to note that the elevator had been called to the top floor the first time the doors were pried open just below that and to respond accordingly by laying himself against the door-side wall—still four or five stories below. The beam of light did not make it to the shaft floor, thus the inspection was unsuccessful. But it seemed to have stopped at the spring plate in the center of the floor, which was only three feet from Rett. That was far enough—at least for now.

The second time was easier, as they'd sent the elevator all the way to the basement level, which was but inches above the prone Rett James, while they examined the upper shaft. For that one, Rett was well hidden by the elevator itself from the hunting eyes, searching flashlights, and pointing guns.

But there might be a third time. And if they use a different tactic of sending the elevator high, but prying open the door at basement level and searching from there? Well, Rett James was right there and could not be missed.

Not by examining searching eyes. Not by a gun. Rett had friends who were DSS, some who were GRS, and had met Secret Service-types, and he considered it very likely that this was a tactic they would employ.

Rett considered the odds about 80%.

That meant there was a 20% chance they might not.

A 20% chance he might not be discovered in this shaft that had obviously never been cleaned—the floor was so grimy it was like dirt.

A 20% chance, then, that he might survive.

Might.

Hiding from the gunmen for days now gave him a far better chance of survival than an open gunfight would.

Carrying a gun also imbues the armed person with an unearned confidence. Gives him a false sense of power. A false sense of hope. This allows for a skewed analysis, allowing them to consider to themselves, *Oh, I'm sure I'll be just fine.*

Additionally, men with guns tend to attach their egos to it and mistake confidence for skill.

Just like every man (male) you ask will proudly tell you he is the best driver, every man (male) thinks himself superior to Annie Oakley (who was not a male).

Every single one of them is wrong.

So, not possessing a gun is a pragmatic approach to not allowing that flaw of ego bias into the analysis.

Plus, a gunfight would only confirm the theory that the hypothetical atrocity was a planned operation.

(Note—do not use the word 'assassination.' That is illegal.)

A coordinated targeted fatal attack on three key individuals—all three of whom had very much in common. All in the same place, within hours of each other, and by the same method.

Though, to be sure, the official causes of death would likely not be exactly the same, since whichever vital organ failed first could not be predicted (which is one way ricin is convenient). In fact, results would be so random as to not even suggest any related method. Nor would any postmortem reveal the presence of ricin. Unless the specifically issued ventilator or oxygen tubing was tested, it would never be detected (even if it could, this unique micro-encapsulated version was non-attributable).

And the chance any tubing would be tested is near zero. Hospitals don't store or reuse disposable issued equipment like that. It quickly becomes medical waste, mixed into copious amounts of other medical waste, then incinerated.

The only real evidence then that such an atrocity, such an operation, might have occurred is the actual people involved in it. And, as long as they aren't caught, they'll never talk.

Getting caught, however, whether in this hospital now or elsewhere a decade from now, is a different matter altogether. This government, this family, is very experienced in forcing people to talk.

Often their last words.

So, Rett would push hard to squeeze out every drop of that 20% chance of survival. Even in this elevator shaft.

No matter how long it took.

He hadn't planned on 54 hours spanning over a period of four calendar days, but this was the hand he was dealt.

A 20% chance of survival.

He didn't know then, that it wasn't enough.

A MOMENT TO DREAM

...

Here's an important tip.

If you ever plan on taking a very long flight, or expect an extremely long day where a bathroom break might be problematic, do not eat anything but concentrated nutrient foods for a couple days prior and drink as little liquid as possible.

A chase or serious fight is a really bad time to discover your bladder demands attention. The human body can withstand a bit of dehydration. Prior to the event, cut the carbs completely. No fiber either. Think Atkins, if you have to. If the matter will be intense, well-timed stimulants help. This is not dietary advice on how to live a healthy lifestyle. This isn't a long-term thing. This is simply optimizing game-day performance without distractions.

Minus the stimulants, the same preparation holds true for spending a completely unforeseen (probably unforeseeable) 54 hours spanning four days at the bottom of an elevator shaft so as to avoid getting violently killed and made into an international incident similar to those which have triggered world wars.

Same advice.

It sounds as if four days is a long time to not eat or drink anything. But it just sounds like it. Saying 'four days,' as it will become in multiple retellings (partial retellings, that is—with all the classified bits removed) sounds like utter starvation.

But it really isn't.

Two reasons: One—it was only 54 hours that happened to span four days on a calendar.

Two—after a while, about 30 hours or so, hunger pains seem to subside. It's an odd thing to think that after a while, you're just not hungry anymore. But it's a strange truth.

But, again, what does happen are a constant flood of sometimes very deep thoughts, self-reflection, life-evaluation, planning, and even examination of the cognitive process itself.

An entire lifetime (in this case, 31 years of it, anyway) can be examined in 54 hours (or more dramatically, four days).

Four days without sleep. (Minus a few careless moments of micro-sleep.)

That, too, affects thoughts and the process of it, obviously. Still, the thoughts flow.

This wasn't supposed to happen. Rett, alone now, had no idea of the fate of the rest of his team. And he had no idea what they were thinking of his fate or doing. What if they'd been captured? Any one of the six could be spilling the beans right now about any of the other five—plus the few recruited as support. Any of that recruited support could also be spilling the same beans about what they knew. The one piece of common intel all of them had was Rett. All threads led to him. While some of the support people didn't know Rett's real name, he and his interpreter had met personally. Aliases and half-established back-stopping was definitely not guaranteed protection. Eventually, every thread can be traced, every knot untied, every secret uncovered. This can even lead all the way back to family. While most countries won't do it, some countries consider the families of a hostile operative to be fair game. This country and family, since that was a large part of this operation itself, would definitely not be above such retaliatory measures.

What that means is Rett's actions, as birthed by the well-intended white paper, put his very own family at risk, and they'd never know it. Others' families as well. Often without anyone even realizing the full picture. Not knowing what they were doing or why—or even to whom.

At some point, it will be discovered that the electronic medical records of two of the targeted royal men had been tampered with, hacked by some force who was skilled enough to penetrate a near-impenetrable system. There aren't many organizations which could. Among them was Cicada. A thread which followed could lead inevitably to Egg—then to Rett.

At some point, there might have been actual witnesses to the triangulated targeting of at least two of the royals by the microwave-cannon wielders, no matter how well disguised the directed energy psychotronic weapons were. A connection could be made linking the acute (and even lingering) symptoms of the targeted royals to their sudden medical consultations, opening the door to the medical record manipulations, which led to secondary manipulated consultations, manipulated diagnostics, manipulated lab work, manipulated diagno-ses, and even manipulated scheduling, placing them here—for the final touch.

Any such eyewitnesses to the psychotronic-wielders could

alert suspicions. Connections found, traced back to the U.S., back to their families, and more link-analysis results culminating in a singular common figure. Rett James.

After days in the dark, Rett had no idea if those connections were being made, even now.

Selfish, in a way.

In part, the leverage for all this was the opportunity for Rett to secure the financing he needed to save his company. A company which was only jeopardized in the first place by his own poor decision-making to save a buck. How long would—how long could—Rett drag such a thing out? How long would he prolong the incepted demise of a doomed product line of a company becoming obsolete?

This is a lesson that his mother's life should have taught him. His mother was a photographer. In the 1960s and '70s, that was a very competitive business. Each local market had its own established and well-known photographers who protected their local monopoly as if it were its own royal family. There was no way to meaningfully penetrate the professional photography marketplace in those days, so Rett's mother settled into a very lucrative niche—next-day photo booths.

What she was capitalizing on was that every family had several cameras, but no photo lab in their house to develop the film from those cameras. A city of 100,000—which might have been dominated by three professional photographers charging a premium—was actually filled with 99,997 amateur photographers who needed their personal film developed quickly and replaced with a new, fresh reel of 35mm, 110, or whatever kind of camera they used. These tiny next-day photo booths—each the size of a small bathroom—would be strategically placed, usually in the visible middle of a busy shopping center parking lot. And would capture that 99,000+.

Rett's mother, then, was still in the photography business. Not in the way she'd always dreamed of, perhaps, but still an integral part of it. She didn't own her own photo lab or dark room. At the end of each day, she'd simply FedEx all the dropped-off customer film rolls to a massive contracted photo lab, which would FedEx the developed photos right back to her once printed.

For almost three decades—the '70s, '80s, and '90s, at least most of it—this was an incredibly lucrative business. Then, the pharmacy chains began stepping into the business, causing a competitive tightening. The knock-out blow to the photomat business came in the form of digital photography. Digital cameras and printers replaced the old click-and-advance film boxes that people had been used to for a century. Within but five years of the first big digital camera surge, a century of tradition and multiple industries which comprised the tradition were killed.

Even the spy business. Even the first TENCAP-era spy satellites operated like the high-altitude spy planes with film-operated cameras, clicking at the terrain below. The full film canister was ejected, reentered Earth's atmosphere, and would parachute safely (hopefully) to the ground, awaiting retrieval by some intelligence service's techie, no matter where it landed.

Rett should have learned from his mother's experience that once the writing was on the wall that a product would become extinct, then there was a point of diminished returns which should act as the stop-loss option.

But Rett was stubborn. And loyal. (Is that the same thing?) And eLocity was his baby. And who just gives up their baby?

One thing his mother did instill in him was a need to know and appreciate philosophy. He actually thought all mothers did the same for their sons or daughters. One he ranked highly was Nietzsche. But, in this case, he could not fully subscribe to Nietzsche's idea—"That which is falling should be pushed."

Rett tended to hold onto things.

While there is some good to that, it is also maladaptive when it causes one to be stuck in an elevator shaft in 2002, in a hostile place, in order to not get shot for (hypothetically) committing a serious treaty violation, a war crime atrocity.

A red line has to be drawn somewhere. Don't cross that red line. Apparently, Rett was colorblind.

This wasn't supposed to happen.

Such desperate measures to right his sinking ship were made acceptable by his imbalanced propensity to not let go. In this sense, Rett James was the moral equivalent of a hoarder. Only, instead of holding on to physical stuff, he clung to principles and ideas even when out of fashion.

Again, some might call that loyalty.

Some, though, just call it stubborn.

The hyper-patriotism of the post-9/11 world fed the logic behind the it's-either-us-or-them sentiment. Compounded by vengeance, which was the currency of the day, that meant more things for Rett James to hold on to and justify his chronic behavior for—the ends justify the means—resulting frequently in risk-taking behavior.

Other people, normal people, didn't have to deal with

moments like this. Or with ruminations like this. They could keep their lives simple. Simple and happy. He envied that.

And yet, even when he had the simple and uncomplicated life he now envied, he had usually found creative ways to make it more complicated. Wanting more and too quickly, not carefully.

Rett James was a detail-oriented, meticulous planner, to be sure. But isn't much of the success of life about timing? A cautious, measured, and well-timed pace often beats a highly orchestrated, highly coordinated, hyper-organized rush.

Those problems come from, again, working out the *how* before considering the *why*. Imposing values onto others through tricks and tactics of leadership is no moral high ground. In fact, it is a moral hazard. It is well within a man's right to stand firm on what he believes and then act upon it. But he has no moral license to risk others' lives and fortunes without their obvious acceptance and even concurrence. That's reckless.

Yet it happens every day.

Especially so in the arrogant world of intelligence operations, where most links in the operational chain never know the big picture or ask the *why* of things—because of adherence solely to the generalized and non-specific tenet of 'need to know.'

Very prevalent in this field. And it is unnatural. It may be the perfect place for it, but it's unnatural.

Imagine this: A husband comes home and tells the family, "We're moving to Hackensack." Obviously, he'd be asked why.

How acceptable would his answer be if he said, "Well

you don't need to know. Just get rid of all your stuff and get in the car"?

Not acceptable at all, to most.

And yet, those that followed Rett into this did so because they'd bought in. The phrase 'buy in' means 'don't question it.' The usual reason someone doesn't want something questioned is because there is no logical answer, or that someone is straight up hiding the truth—or lying.

'Buy in' and 'don't question' are the kinds of things which cult leaders tell their gullible followers just before the Kool-Aid is poured.

The difference here is that Rett James didn't have gullible followers. Any team member was free to reason what and how he chose to, or could simply ask. The trust was placed in Rett, but it was always an earned trust, not a blind trust. That's some consolation.

But not much.

Most people, particularly most Americans, were safely and happily at home. He'd like that, too. His happy moments of sitting on his plush couch watching *Win Ben Stein's Money* with his shih tzu on his lap were moments worth living. Moments worth re-experiencing as frequently as possible.

Not this.

It is frequently said, often accredited to General Patton, "No plan ever survives first contact with the enemy."

Rett had only coordinated the delivery of the laced oxygen tubing for two of the targeted royals, meaning that to the best of his knowledge, the job was only 2/3 complete.

That means it was, to his mind, a bust. But to regroup and salvage something from it, he needed to safely escape.

He was weak beyond all description, his head was pounding, he was extremely disoriented from lack of fluids and lack of sleep, and four days of adrenaline had finally taken its toll. For better or worse, it was time for him to emerge.

It may be part of the hunters' passive search or third phase to simply wait for exactly this moment. Watching each patient as they are released with family members, possibly presuming that the likely culprit had the best chance of hiding all this time in a patient's room as an actual patient. All the in-and-out staff had already been checked multiple times.

Rett tried to stand on two stiff but shaking legs. As a hand-to-hand combat instructor, Rett had competed up to the elite level in taekwondo for over a decade, but at this moment, there was no chance of him trying a jump-spin 360-degree sidekick. He'd be lucky to manage a semi-normal walk. A slight crack at the top of the rear service elevator door allowed him to find his fingers along to feel where the door itself was. While the elevator was somewhere above him, he had time. He hit the tiny light button on his calculator watch. It was 3:20 a.m.

Over 53 hours.

It was now or never.

Stretching out to catch the release, Rett felt that side of the double door permit him to move it. This was normally a simple task, as the springs are intentionally not strong. But, at that moment, it felt Herculean.

The good news is that the movement was silent.

Rett had chosen the back door of the basement shaft because it was the only floor which had one. Also, because this is where he'd left his 'bug out' bundle.

After a few inches, welcome fresh air brushed his face.

He peered into the hallway cautiously to ensure it was clear. It was.

The passage bent sharply to the right and Rett could lean his head through far enough to see the dimly lit underbelly of the hospital. The coast was clear. Another reason this was the perfect place to emerge.

Getting both arms through the door and reaching up to the floor of the basement to pull himself up, while fighting the door from closing, was a tremendous effort. Rett noticed then, in the dim lighting, how blackened his arms had become from the filth. Then, a huffing crawl upward and through. Rett saw it was not just his arms, but the whole of him.

As the door closed behind him, he inhaled the air hungrily, coughing out the grime. Realizing he had to move, he shuffled down the hallway to where he knew a tiny bathroom was. Its door scraped the floor as he pushed it inward. Obviously seldom used. He lurched for the sink, aching for water.

He spun the faucets on. Nothing.

He looked under the sink—maybe the sink lines were turned off at the valves. But there were no valves. No lines.

The plumbing had been removed from this sink. Probably for over a decade.

Desperate times called for desperate measures.

He flung open the toilet bowl lid.

Empty.

He struggled to lift the lid from the tank.

Empty.

He hit the flush lever to start a water flow.

Nothing.

Figures.

This is often how life goes. The road between life point A and life point B is loaded with hellish, bloody thorns of unimaginable deterrents. This, Rett imagined, is exactly why so few deign to move from life point A once familiarity becomes comfort.

For most, the incentives to overcome the powerful influence of comfort require far more than some mere possibility of improvement of life's conditions. In fact, often the driving impetus for decisions (of the comfort-altering kind, particularly) is fear—which is one of the most powerful motivators.

Rett James, however, didn't seem to require such dramatic, amygdalic influence to color his decision-making, as applied to quantifiable measures of risky ventures—the kind of perilous provocations against comfort which would make his characterization either intrepid or suicidal (whichever, being determined by the outcome).

Rett didn't consider himself either of those. In his mind, he simply does what needs doing without any measurable consideration of safety or comfort—or ultimate consequence.

Usually he wins.

But, in life, the losses—even if but a small percentage—carry the most weight and even paint a person's legacy. It is as if the scribe of personal reputation, and of life's station, hardly records the successes, but boldfaces and underlines the failures.

They say that failure builds character.

Of course that's true, but so do the successes. You do learn (hopefully) from mistakes, but you learn more from success. That reality however, doesn't sell as well on motivational posters or make for a good bumper sticker.

Reflecting on success is considered bad social form, lacking humility.

Interesting thing though, immediately after a boxing match, it isn't the loser who is interviewed. It is the victor.

Humility for the sake of social appeasement is false.

No one can learn from false humility. It not only has no positive value, but it has a *negative* value.

Regardless, for Rett to consider this operation a success (which was a notion becoming more elusive by the moment) would require him to find a way to flip this around from failure. Step one, from this point, is survival.

Though he'd been suffering while still in the shaft, he wasn't doing anything active to change the situation—not flipping it, merely mitigating potential loss. Out of the shaft, now, he needed to rehydrate, reenergize, and reassess.

OODA. Observe (current situation). Orient (recognize where you are in the situation, so as to plan). Decide. Act.

There was no water here. And he was entirely exposed. Anyone could come along at any moment. Even a hunter.

He hurried down hallways that he'd forgotten he'd previously memorized and somehow found himself going deeper into the subterranean labyrinth complex instead of out of it. A large, darkened room he entered was dimly lit by a single fluorescent fixture. It had one dim tube lit and the other was flashing off with a stuttering frequency. The room was stacked high with unmaintained equipment. Multiple automatic hospital beds that had been stripped of various parts. Rolling IV poles which had been similarly stripped out. Wheelchairs missing wheels. Obsolete lab machines and diagnostic equipment that had long since been updated. Eerily, a few CPR certification dummies sat atop a retired salad bar. Multiple television sets, in various states of disrepair littered the room, piled atop other detritus—including an ancient Coca-Cola machine in the corner, unplugged and standing slightly crooked.

Within seconds, Rett had crossed through the hoarded junk and pulled at the door of the dead Coke machine. The locked front didn't budge. The machine had been retired for at least 20 years, given its basic style and logo. There was even a selection for 'New Coke' as well as 'Classic Coke' which definitely dated this thing to the days of Rett's childhood. He was very familiar with this era of machine.

The front door of it was still locked.

Hmm—

The wide dispensing mouth did not fight against Rett's arm as he desperately fell to his knees and reached up at an angle through the flap, as his fingers lifted it and his arm wiggled deeper.

This had been much easier back when he was a child. The arm of an eleven or twelve-year-old is a much better fit for Coke-machine thievery than that of a weakened 31-year-old man.

All of this was but a mindless moment of hope (desperation?) in Rett's given situation. But back in his younger days, it was more a matter of him wondering if he can do it.

A great many deeds are the result of the wonder-if-you-can type of moment.

Some of those good. Some decidedly bad. Some are a matter of perspective. Like a kid with a new gun wondering if he can hit that bird might lead to the outcome of a family enjoying an interesting stew later that night—a good outcome for the family, but not for the bird.

In Rett's case, it was all bad.

He had once hit the bird and it fluttered to the ground, dying. Rett then felt guilty and had no intention of defeathering or cooking the bird for supper and didn't even tell his mother about it. She was a horrible cook anyway and wouldn't have known what to do except chastise her son, since she was an avid birdwatcher and photographer. To make matters worse, when he went to investigate the downed bird, he was attacked, dive-bombing style, by the lightning-fast swooping mate of the one he'd shot! No one was happy. Not Rett. Not the dead bird victim, certainly. And not the bird victim's family, who probably chattered to all the other birds about Rett's viciousness.

I wonder if I can... is an emergent phenomenon of childhood curiosity. It was what led to Rett's well-secreted ability to pick locks (or open locked doors, which isn't always quite the same as picking the actual lock itself). When Rett was only 5 years old (1976), he'd learned how to open locked doors by opening his parents' locked home office in their home in Texas.

Why?

Because that's where his father's globe was, and Rett had to get to it. Rett's mother, to satisfy the natural, yet unnatural, curiosity of her aberrant son had given him a globe of his own. But it wasn't enough for him. His was a small one, which doubled as a piggy bank, complete with a coin slot at the Arctic and a rubber plug under the un-swiveling base of Antarctica. Rett needed to get to the real globe. The one that stood as tall as he was and swiveled and spun. Every country was clearly printed and all the oceans, seas, and major lakes labeled. The lines of latitude and longitude clearly delineated. The degree of tilt and the time compass haloed the top of it. Everything a future satellite CEO would long for. All the stuff a five-year-old would demand.

Why did he have to get to it?

Because it was there.

(As was the giant digital calculator, which sat atop the desk and plugged into the 110-volt socket, as calculators did in 1976.)

So, there was little chance that a locked door would stop a curious five-year-old boy in 1976.

There was little chance that the odd alignment of angles of a Coke machine's path of can-dispensing would stop an eleven-year-old who was thinking *I wonder if I can* in 1982.

And so, at the moment, in 2002, Rett James felt he'd willingly sacrifice his much larger adult arm to retrieve whatever can was inside of this now antiquated, decommissioned machine.

This machine had not been empty when it stopped working, however many years ago that was. Rett confirmed this as his fingers touched more than the stacks that were in reach. At least the stacks on either side of the center held the weight of likely two or three cans.

The maneuver was a simple one once your fingertips could gain control of the front can. From all his practice in childhood, without thinking, he tilted the bottom can, nose-down to clear the bar; then he simply pulled.

The can, if it held, would come out dented, but once it was

halfway, it would pull right out. Once free, it was a matter of just getting your stuck arm out of the way and unstuck.

That part wasn't easy. But, with tight red indentations and scratches across his filthy, blackened arm, Rett was able to reclaim his now sore limb and claim his prize as it fell into the mouth of the machine.

A Mello Yello.

Under normal circumstances, it is not advisable to drink a warm Mello Yello that is dusty and two decades old. The soda was, literally, more than half Rett's age. Such advice against doing this accounts even for the curiosity factor and equates with asking himself, *I wonder what dry cat food tastes like.*

But it was still liquid and still contained sugar. This was not a normal circumstance. Nor should it be forgotten that only minutes earlier, Rett James was perfectly willing to tolerate toilet water, excusing it as a do-or-die decision, until he discovered there was no such water to drink. So, in a life-or-death situation, accommodations must be made (or, at least in this life-or-death situation, especially since no one would ever know about it). Alas, in the end, submitting to a dusty old Mello Yello would be better than submitting to toilet water (but, even if the toilet water had actually existed, any future retelling of it would replace that with a geriatric Mello Yello).

Regardless of the taste or quality of the alleged fluid, it was still liquid and still calories. Rett could feel the energy returning to even his fingertips. It began as a between-the-fingers tingle and quickly spread to his entire body, allowing him to breathe in hope for the first time in four days.

Still, he wasn't thinking right and lost track of where he'd placed his 'bug out' go pack down here. By 3:58 a.m., he had found the one double-door exit from the basement level, which he knew led up a short ramp to a side alley where the mortician would pick up the expired—just as two had been shuttled from here just four days ago. Now, at 4:00 in the morning, there was no guard and no paperwork to sign before reaching this exit. Just a bar across the door and a placard stating that an alarm would sound if opened.

Rett doubted that warning to be true, but he did consider that the hunters would definitely be watching this door, or at least the alleyway, for an unauthorized vehicle.

He decided to forgo his 'bug out' bag and the well-planned slip-out disguise that was in it, wherever it was, and opted instead to avail himself of the here-and-now opportunity of this door, right there.

He knew that he couldn't use a regular exit on the ground floor since the actual elevator cars did have active cameras, and getting to a ground floor exit where people were, he'd not only be noticed, but would be very noticeable.

A European-looking man with a short, stubbly beard and coated in filth? People would remember that.

No. This exit from the basement, up the ramp and into the alleyway, was far too tempting to pass up. He must use this moment. And if there are bad guys with guns (although, who exactly is the bad guy here?) on the other side, well, then he'd have to run. Or hobble, really. As fast as he could (which at the moment, probably wouldn't be that fast).

As it turns out, the alarm on the doors actually did work, but that only caused Rett to sprint the alleyway to the corner, then turn left and walk out as if all was normal. Away from the hospital.

If there was anyone in the alleyway, he didn't even see them.

At the point where Rett had made it two blocks away, his hope lifted as he recalculated his chance of survival now getting higher. Not great odds yet, but better.

Then, a few blocks further away, he began to simultaneously think, *Okay, now what?* and also noticed that there were no cars on the streets, an observation he'd hoped was merely due to the time.

The one person he'd seen, who was unlocking a bakery across the street from his random path, glanced at him oddly—which reminded him that he probably looked like a mess of a destitute homeless bum in the middle of a very rich city, which had no destitute homeless bums (especially in that section of the city). Accordingly, Rett became conscientious about his appearance, walking in shadows so as to not be noticed. Despite his clarity and mission-focus, he'd never been more terrified in his life.

He planned where he needed to go and checked the stored number in the memory of his calculator watch, which was really but an address.

By the time the sun was up and the city's morning activities were underway—as announced by the call to prayer—Rett had arrived at a single-story, gated apartment complex, slipped past the gate, and was knocking on a specific door.

He arrived at precisely the right moment, almost.

"Dr. Oli?" Rett said in English, as the door swung open to reveal a short Arabic man, long-bearded and wide-eyed.

"Come in! Now!" Oli replied.

Rett stumbled through the doorway as Oli chastised him, "Do not speak English out there!"

Rett collapsed onto the man's living room floor. "I'm sorry. I wasn't thinking."

"What has happened? Why are you still in this city? They're looking for you! They're stopping every car with a European in it. Even Persian. What happened to you? Why did you come here? To *me*!?!"

"I didn't know where else to go," Rett answered. "Long story."

"I—I'll get you some tea, water, food. You get cleaned up. Rest. I'll have my assistant teach classes today."

Rett's eyes closed. "No. Go. Teach classes as if nothing is going on. Do nothing out of the ordinary. I'll rest here and clean up. I may even be gone by the time you get back."

"Okay," Dr. Oli replied, "There's some biryani in the chiller. I doubt my clothes will fit, but you can try. Should I call or contact anyone?"

"Can you access Protonmail from the university?"

"What? What is that?"

"Damn. Okay—umm—what about ordinary Hotmail?"

"Hotmail. Yes."

"Okay," Rett struggled to sit up. "Give me a pen."

Two minutes later, Dr. Oli was locking up his apartment as if leaving for the day. The slip of paper in his pocket held the instructions Rett had written for him.

A quick shower preceded a cup of cold long-rice biryani and a deep nap on the floor (to enhance the drama of it, future retellings would leave out the nap part).

Dr. Oli had said "stopping every car" and "looking for Europeans or Persians." Rett had no Persian-looking men on the team. This implies the hunters deeply suspected something, and had the clout to call in serious resources but didn't quite know what or who they were looking for exactly.

But, Rett knew the affected family, by reputation anyway.

And he knew they'd probably never stop. Never.

But for now, a moment to dream.

ABOVE IT

...

By late afternoon, just past Asr, Professor Oli had returned to his apartment with a long, printed email reply, for which Rett chastised him for carrying on his person.

"Imagine if you'd been caught with this!"

"I may yet still be," confessed Oli. "University computer activity might be very easy to trace. But, I couldn't memorize all this from your friend from the north. I *did*, however, memorize the response back from your other friends. Just a time and an address."

Rett nodded, "That means a meeting. How much time do I have?"

"About three hours," Oli replied.

"Okay. That may be time enough," Rett noted as he reviewed the long email. "My friend has put together a risky but brilliant plan. Do you have a map?"

"This is 2002," Oli huffed, "I can print any map you want from the internet."

"No," Rett shook his head, "a paper map. We can't have you leaving a search history on your computer using your IP address."

"I have some. They may be older, but I do. What are we looking for? What are we trying to find?"

"Not finding, really. Placing and hiding. Fueling locations. I'll need some vehicles loaded discretely with fuel on regular stops—"

Oli laid out several maps, "Okay—*we* are here, obviously," he pointed.

"Okay then," Rett's finger traced a line. "While I'm gone, I'll need you to coordinate the stationing and hiding of fuel at specific coordinates along *this* line, kind of parallel to it."

"To this highway? Toward Jordan?" Oli shook his head. "They are watching the highways. Probably looking for you. Especially *that* one! That is a very long way to Jordan. The highway is fast, but a bad idea."

"I won't be on the highway, Dr. Oli. I'm going above it!"

HOW?

• • •

THE MEETING LATER THAT night proved to be wise caution on the part of Rett's team. He was ecstatic to see that this member of his team was actually alive, but concerned that they had not yet escaped this city, this country. It was difficult for Rett to curtail his reaction upon seeing Jeff.

Jeff was cautious in ensuring that Rett hadn't been followed and instead of greeting Rett, silently began an SDR path back toward one of the alternate safe-house locations. Rett kept his distance, but followed the same route.

Once inside the extremely cramped space, Rett's face lit up and his eyes couldn't help but swell with tears. "Oh my god, you're all alive!"

"You're alive!" Alan proclaimed, just as giddy. "And you look like hell! Where have you been?"

"Long story," Rett prefaced before filling the other five in. As they all debriefed each other, he learned that they had been successful—kind of. Three out of three.

The third royal who was supposed to be rushed to the hospital following a staged car crash actually died in the crash itself!

One of the royals' death had been caused by a very rare complication ("random organ failure") occurring during a scheduled routine appendectomy. An appendectomy that hadn't really been needed, but advised after sudden symptoms occurred and a consulting surgeon reviewed the chief complaints and lab work.

The second royal had suddenly complained of odd, overwhelming symptoms, then in consult and post-lab work, was briefly placed on oxygen. He died within 48 hours with the bizarre and unheard-of postmortem diagnosis of "thirst."

And the third had died at the scene of the crash that had been organized to send the man to the hospital, where Rett had been waiting and hiding.

"So that's why I only got 2 out of 3," Rett said. "The third guy never made it!"

"He probably *did* make it," Alan noted. "But he was already dead when he got there."

"What about your demolition driver?" Rett inquired.

"Well," Alan squinted. "He's not going to be a problem for us."

Rett nodded. Sometimes losses happen. Recruited assets know the risks they take, usually. But still, they are people. Valuable people. But now was not the right moment to spend dealing with that loss.

"Now we go home," Rett announced.

"How?" Alan inquired. "The hospital was locked down while you were in it! The city is on alert. The airports are at heightened security and all the roads out are being seriously watched. We've been just as stuck as you were in that elevator."

Nice try, but not quite.

Alan continued, "Jeff took a hell of a risk just going out to meet you. We can't contact the COS here, as you know, and we can't coordinate with HQ. We can't just steal a car and drive home."

"No," Rett smiled, scratching at his annoying beard, which he was eager to get rid of. "We aren't stealing a car."

"Then what do we do?" John #2 asked.

"We steal a helicopter," Rett answered. "And, you're gonna fly it!"

GO

...

THE IMPROMPTU PLAN WAS explained to the group and not even questioned. This isn't quite what Rett expected. He'd been prepared to defend the details, each one. The mood was odd. Indescribable.

The other five seemed subdued, almost as if they had completely detached themselves from the moment. Maybe the gravity of what was being done—and what they'd actually accomplished—was overwhelming. This was definitely too much for a normal person.

But these were not normal people.

Not now. Especially not now.

A line had been crossed that could never be uncrossed.

This is a line that sears into a man's very soul, not like a permanent tattoo—more like a brand.

A part of them, it seemed, felt as if they shouldn't be alive.

In truth, maybe a part of them had died.

They were just waiting on the rest of themselves to follow.

People talk about revenge as a medicine. Those who do so haven't really tried doing much more than talking. It is no medicine. It certainly has no therapeutic effect. Not even placebic.

Revenge is empty. It is nothing.

It is like blowing smoke into a glass, expecting it to stay. It doesn't. It soon wisps away, dissipating into nothing—because that's all it ever was. It provides no satisfaction whatsoever.

Officially, that wasn't the purpose. Officially, the Bush Doctrine—"… if you support terrorism, you'll be treated as one in our war against it"—gave the green light to ensure these three men were incapable of funding Al-Qaeda operations through Al Dhalam Ledger networks. Officially, it would send a chilling message to other would-be terrorism supporters or funders.

But officially, this entire thing never happened. Leaving only the *unofficially*.

Revenge.

These six men would have to wait in emptiness—sitting in it, marinating in it—until their extraction moment was ripe.

No. That's not quite right.

There would be no extraction. No one was coming to get them. They'd have to remove themselves.

Rett's plan required waiting until 'Mike,' a very trusted person in the U.S., coordinated multiple and exact fuel drop points not too far from, but along a highway to Jordan.

Six locations.

Rett would receive a 'GO' signal when that was done and that is when the six men would effect their own escape. Rett wasn't certain, but he figured Mike would use a man known to Rett as 'the Hedgehog' to handle the drops, record the precise coordinates, then somehow get those coordinates to Rett. He would receive the coordinates as they were leaving.

The 'GO' signal would simply be a silent answer of Dr.

Oli's mobile phone. That is, after several rings, Dr. Oli would answer by saying nothing for a few seconds before hanging up. This would indicate that the Hedgehog had completed the long drive down from Jordan, stashing fuel along the way, and had made it into the city where Rett and his team were now hidden in silence.

The Hedgehog, if that's who Mike sent, might take days to get it all done. Maybe a week. By the time he finally rolled into town, Rett and the team might be discovered and will have been killed. They were truly on borrowed time.

Five of them had already been in this tiny apartment for four days at least, now joined by Rett. Six now, with no room to think, staying below and out of sight of the one window slightly ajar. Staying near-silent, lest someone overhear their English. It felt like an overcrowded jail cell.

Rett had already had a long four days. Three more days would be a week of adrenaline, but no action. By the time he'd actually needed it, there may be none left, having already depleted his entire lifetime supply.

"Let's rest as much as we can," Jason wisely advised the group. "Preserve our energy."

Rest. Easy for him to say. If by 'rest' Jason meant 'sleep,' then Rett had forgotten what it felt like. Unlike the couple ex-military guys here, Rett didn't have that 'sleep switch' they seem to have. They can turn themselves off and shut themselves down at will, it seems. Rett didn't have that skill.

All Rett knew, now, was sleeplessness. He couldn't yet know he would be in for a lifetime curse of exactly that. He couldn't yet have known it would be a short curse. He couldn't yet know that his life would soon end.

ALONG FOR THE RIDE

. . .

IT HAD TAKEN BARELY a day for the Hedgehog to place all of the makeshift and well-disguised fuel deposits in safe and accessible places, spaced properly. No trace was left behind in the safe house. The six men even took the drain traps from the single sink and bleached every wall and all furniture. The drain trap, bleach, all clothing, and the one blanket in the place, was disposed of just before they stopped two cabs, separately of course—five minutes apart—and made their way to a small airfield near an industrial area by the darker edge of town.

Six men, five minutes apart, arrived just under a small bridge which crossed a ravine. After nearly 45 minutes of waiting, they heard a vehicle stop on the bridge and barely honk its feeble horn.

Rett, himself, stepped out from under the bridge at the deepest part of the still-moist ravine and looked up. A stumpy looking Arabic man made of 200% muscle appeared at the edge of the bridge next to the idling car and looked down. The Hedgehog.

They recognized each other with a slight nod. The

Hedgehog, looking weary, dropped a backpack over the edge. Rett, despite being weary, surprised himself briefly by catching it. When he glanced back up, the Hedgehog was gone. A car door shut and the vehicle revved away with a valve click.

Once again, it was early morning, hours before dawn.

Nothing good comes out at night.

The Hedgehog had included in his backpack not only a written list of coordinates, but a small hand-crank pump, a small cell phone and a tool set with wire cutters—and on the very GPS unit, he'd marked interest points as a point-to-point destination route in the higher-tech navigation system, fully charged. Good for him. Rett was proud that no expense was being spared.

That pride lasted only three minutes.

The ravine itself ran into the small airfield, which was used primarily for repair services. Because of the nature of the work here, none of the planes could really be trusted.

But they weren't breaking into this place for a plane. They were after a helicopter.

First, they had to get past the simple chain-link fence which stretched through the ravine and ran the entire property. That's when the wire cutters proved to be cheap, unreliable, and ineffective.

There was no way to cut through the fence.

The relief came quickly, though, when Jason—kind of a country boy—untwisted the tie-wire from the steel fence post, from the fence itself, and simply lifted the bottom of the fence up, curling it nearly three feet from the ground. High enough for everyone.

And that's it. That simple technique—the technique of

a curious child crawling under a fence—is how a team of highly-trained clandestine operators gained entry into this restricted place.

To steal an air-ambulance that had been (hopefully) repaired.

The Eurocopter 350 is distinctive and unmistakable in appearance, but was easy to find, being that it was the only helicopter under the open hangar.

Pulling the tarp off revealed blue stripes on a white whirlybird.

Six people in a Bell Ranger really wouldn't work. Someone would have to be on someone else's lap and the machine would sluggishly complain even before lift-off.

The Eurocopter 350, however, was a little more accommodating and there was but 45 seconds between when they pulled it from under the roof—thirty feet—and spun up to lift-off. It was cramped inside, but everyone still found a way to fit.

There was no way that this blacked-out unauthorized lift-off would go unnoticed and unreported. This was now a race. And it would take hours.

Getting as much altitude as possible when not near one of the point-to-point coordinates marked in the GPS would cut down on the amount of rotor noise the ground would notice, but not eliminate it. Following it wouldn't be impossible. There would be no hiding from radar either. The movie tactic of 'flying below the radar' is a myth when crossing over a city. It can't happen and would bring even more scrutiny. This was going to be about speed—from point-to-point—and accuracy.

And, in practice, accuracy is the same thing as speed.

Rett sat in back, squished against the door on the far right.

He was useless when it came to helicopters. Along for the ride. And, despite what anyone says, there's no such thing as a smooth helicopter ride. Nor is the Eurocopter 350 exactly the Cadillac of rotary wing vehicles.

Stanick and McCormick could handle it, though—not like there was much choice. If they couldn't, then Alan or Jason could step up. But Rett and Jeff were determined to be passengers. No one was really qualified for this bird, though. One might think that knowing how to fly one helicopter automatically qualifies one for them all. That is very far from reality. Knowing how to drive a go-kart doesn't qualify someone for an 18-wheeler, does it?

That's the analog.

Plus, there is a difference in the intellectualized knowing of procedure versus actual hands-on proficiency.

His experience, Rett thought of himself, should be shameful—considering that he comes from a family of flyers. His grandfather flew iconic B-25 bombers in WWII, his father was a pilot, and his mother was no stranger to the stick either. Rett's Coast Guard veteran stepfather (Coast Guard is very dependent upon helicopters) had tried for years to interest him in the art and skill of at least basic aircraft control, and even built Rett a Lazy Susan glider, which Rett was never able to land safely, much less properly. In fact, over the span of several early-teen years, Rett crashed the glider so frequently that Rett's stepfather eventually got tired of repairing it. This didn't hurt Rett's feelings at all. Rett was interested in the science of it, but taking the stick was never going to be his thing. Proof that the knowing of something does not automatically translate to the actual doing of it.

In adulthood, Rett was told to stick to the simulators. Good advice. Of course, simulators were boring, so he never really stuck with that either. An hour now and then on a simulator is an hour which could have been used actually doing something productive.

And that was just fixed-wing stuff.

Helicopters are an entirely different beast altogether.

There were no expectations that this would be a quick trip, even between drums. But from drum to GPS-coordinated drum was plenty of time to build a deep appreciation for the next opportunity to stretch legs and breathe easier—though adrenaline flow and hyper-vigilance still prevented those mere minutes from being relaxing. The human body, the human brain, the human psyche was not designed to operate for nearly a week at maximum stress.

Neither was the Eurocopter 350.

KIDS

· · ·

Seconds after touchdown, in a relatively small zone that the Hedgehog had cleared (mostly) of larger rocks behind a dilapidated shack—which might have once been a well house—all six men were out of the chopper. Less than thirty seconds after that, they located the drums.

Easy, really. The wheel tracks made by the dolly the Hedgehog had apparently used led into the well house.

The crumbling plywood on two misaligned hinges swung open, revealing a tiny space big enough to contain only the drums and some corroding pipes protruding from the ground at varying lengths no more than a foot each. The pump itself had been removed—probably decades ago.

As with previous stops, the exhausted team knew that simply moving the heavy drums the mere thirty feet from where they were stashed to the waiting thirsty bird was a difficult process involving a leaned rocking of the drum back and forth. Although not entirely full, since JP8 fuel weighs about 7.2 pounds per gallon, a drum of fifty-five gallons weighs just over 400 pounds. Not an easy carry, even for three people, so the wobbling, three-person drum walk sufficed just fine.

"Message Dr. Oli," Rett instructed Jason. "Let him know we're at our last checkpoint."

"Roger that," the ex-Ranger replied.

It's annoying sometimes when those ex-military types hold onto their DOD-speak even after reentering the real world with real people. Rett had once raised this social criticism to point out that the real-world (non-military) population did not need to pepper their language with such pretentious qualifiers of the military (or any other) club and that it's not conversational and only exists within that social group.

"It is exactly the elitist mindset that you accuse me of, only of a different flavor," Rett had once told him. "That's not even in the dictionary."

To which Jason had only shrugged, then a day later plunked a dictionary onto Rett's desk, a single page folded inside it.

Apparently, 'roger' *is* in the dictionary.

Regardless, the message was sent.

"Hell, we're nearly there," Jason said as Jeff pumped and Rett listened. "We could practically walk the rest of the way if we had to."

Jeff, ever the professional, replied, "That'd be a bad idea, so I'm glad we don't have to."

Rett squinted as he saw multiple shadows cross into the clearing. The source being a group of young kids, all boys, who'd found their way to inspect the curious racket. It's not every day that a helicopter lands in the backyard of your neighborhood.

Curiosity is often a dangerous thing. Though the boys didn't speak, or approach more than 50 yards. Their expressions (even from this distance) were not of the happy brand of curiosity. Not the kind of curiosity when one hears an unseen kitten waiting to be rescued from some lonely, fearful peril. This was more like the what-do-we-do-now? kind of facial expression reserved for when a snake is discovered under a bush.

The kids moved off and over the ridge within less than a minute.

"We should hurry," Rett commented.

"I can only pump so fast," Jeff responded. "This'll probably take thirty minutes."

Jason shrugged, "Well, we aren't dead *yet*."

That would soon change.

NEARLY DUE

...

TAKING TO THE AIR for the final leg of the trip—the most important one which would result in their freedom—was the first moment in nearly a week that allowed for a relaxed breath. Rett began thinking that the team might actually survive this mission which 'never happened.'

For a moment, he considered all that he might do upon his return. But then, he remembered what a disaster his life was back at home, on the other side of the planet.

Funny how he was able to plan and execute this most dangerous and insane mission—which would have been considered a suicide mission—and that he now found his way to cheat even that, yet the mission awaiting him at home, the one to patch his life back together, eluded him. He could pull off something like this, but he could not seem to manage all the simple things of life that normal people could do with ease.

A wife whose key to contentment was not within Rett's power. Perhaps that was some sort of divine punishment for his winning her away from her husband in the first place. Or maybe they weren't as estranged as she presented to Rett. Maybe her previous estranged husband also had no clue as to how to tame her. Either way, it was a dilemma Rett had no answer for but must deal with upon his return.

A business which also needed a miracle to save. This was yet another seemingly insurmountable task awaiting his return. Rett knew he needed an answer to that, but he had no clue how to arrive at such an answer but was hoping for miracles. Somehow though, he figured that such a miracle answer would present itself, so he wasn't overly stressed on it.

In fact, he was kind of known for making miracles happen. He thought it was actually something he could count on in those moments when he couldn't see his way through.

He felt, now, as if he was in that moment, so he believed that he was nearly due one of those miracle moments which seemed to fix all the things he couldn't.

He was wrong.

Dead wrong.

CLEAR

. . .

It didn't start as a hum. It didn't start as a vibration. It didn't start as a shudder.

It instantly went from a smooth lift-off—which felt almost routine now—to a full-blown violent shake.

Imagine being inside of a paint-mixing shaker.

Then imagine that shaker being inside of a derailing train.

Then imagine that derailing train caught in a deep cliff avalanche, in the midst of a tornado.

It was like that.

Machines aren't made to tolerate that.

A helicopter is a machine.

This helicopter could not survive that.

It didn't.

Rett had seconds to register his thoughts.

Obviously, his first thoughts were, *This is a problem. We aren't supposed to be shaken all around in here so violently. This is so bad that we cannot control our own limbs, so there is no hope in controlling this helicopter. This is quite an abnormality. It seems as though we are all likely to perish.*

His next thoughts were—strangely enough—about his beloved cat, Victoria. Being dead and all means he will not get the chance to retrieve her from his mother's home, where she was waiting. He wasn't too sure Victoria would like to live the rest of her life out in the country as she was much more of an ultra-pampered city cat. Nor was he certain that his mother was terribly fond of the all-white Angora. She was too posh and pretty for his mother's Americanized tastes. Too perfect. His promise to both his mother and to Victoria that he'd bring her to live in Tupelo with him would be broken—on account of him being dead and all. He hoped both his mother and Victoria would forgive him.

One thing about sudden fatal demise is that all these thoughts, no matter how complex and deep, occur in an instant. As if a lifetime of deep thoughts (shallow ones too, really) all suddenly realized that this was their only chance, so they all flood out at once, but are still not the least bit confusing. Everything is so clear, despite the compressed time. This is one way in which we can be certain that time is not a real dimension, merely a perception. An effect, at best. There is no 'fourth dimension of time,' but this helps us try to make sense of the world since our organic understanding is through our senses, and sorting out the elements comprising our understanding, even what 'understanding' itself means, requires tools.

Animals (whether one agrees or not, plants too) require some cognitive tools to process input, whichever way they're programmed to do so, and time is one of those critical conceptual tools that brains cannot do without.

But, an animal brain in peril doesn't obey the standard

processing rules. So, in quantum fashion, it processes things all at once.

Even this was among Rett's final thoughts as he realized they were going to crash, despite that it'd only been 23.4 seconds since they lifted off of the ground.

His last thought was a case study in cynicism.

It figures.

A MOTHER'S DUTY

...

FAR AWAY, A WHITE cordless telephone rang.

It was not in its charging cradle; it had been taken to the front solarium and was sitting on the small craft table which had been turned into a smoking table. The solarium is the one place in her house where Sharon allowed herself to smoke, so she did. A lot.

The rationale for smoking only here was to prevent everything in her house from smelling like cigarettes. The rationale for smoking? Well, that was just a habit.

Smoking at the solarium table allowed her to be still. Being still allowed her to think. And so she did. A lot.

Usually, it was depressing thoughts. People who smoke alone in little square solariums aren't overwhelmed with happiness. They are rarely cheerful. They are very reflective and bad memories cast a strong reflection. Reflective smokers alone in solariums never call a friend and cheerfully prompt, "Hey! Guess what!"

They wait for the phone to ring instead.

Sharon answered, "Hello?"

Smoke billowed over the phone, lingering as if afraid to

leave the familiarity of her stained lungs and contemplating how to get back in. But then, it faded into the air—one more element added into the gasses of the atmosphere.

"Hello?" the other voice queried, probing. Some calls take a lot of courage to make. There's a momentum to build. This was one of those.

The man introduced himself to Sharon. Jody—he said his name was, and that he worked with Sharon's son and was one of his friends. So, she realized that his name may not really be Jody. Those people are liars, all of them. You can't believe anything they say, if they even say anything— which is only half of what they should say, and even that half is cherry-picked and spun. So this man on the phone wasn't to be believed.

"Ma'am, there's been an accident. Your son was involved. He is missing."

"An accident, Mr. Jody?"

"Yes, ma'am."

Accident my ass! "What sort of accident?" she asked.

"I don't know the details, ma'am. I just—"

"If you don't know the details, Mr. Jody, then how can you call it an accident?"

"Uhh—good point. But, I'm calling to tell you as a friend of his, and that he's missing. But I've been asked to ask you not to make any inquiries until we can find out more. Please don't try to call or contact him."

"Missing? from where?"

"These details are sketchy right now, ma'am. I've already probably said more than I should."

"Was he driving that little sports car?"

"No ma'am, nothing like that. I can't confirm it, but it may have been a helicopter."

That, she could believe. "My son can't fly a helicopter. He's a lousy pilot."

"Umm—yes ma'am."

Irritated and heartbroken, she forced, "Is my son alive?"

Pause.

"I—I am told that he is missing. But—mmm—presumed dead."

Another one lost.

She believed him.

"What do I do?" She really was asking herself aloud. Maybe she was asking God. It already felt as if everything had been already been taken from her. There was nothing left for her now.

But a mother's duty.

To clean up after her son.

And to try to pick up whatever remnants of her heart remained.

And smoke another cigarette. Another pack.

"There's really not much you can do, ma'am," Jody answered through a tight, painful throat, thinking her question was actually for him.

Not really hearing his answer, not really remembering she was even on the phone, she muttered, "I'll have to call his Nana. She's going to be heartbroken."

"Ma'am, it's better if you talk to no one about this. Just—wait until I can find out more. I'll—try to learn everything I can and keep you posted. Just wait for me to contact you back."

"Keep me posted!?! This isn't some... 'Sit rep.' This is my *life*. My son's life."

She didn't remember hanging up the phone. She didn't remember thanking him for his call. All she remembered was that she once had a son. A living, breathing, real son. She remembered that.

Now she doesn't.

There were no tears left in her for this.

Tears don't even do the trick. Not enough.

She lit another cigarette.

The smoke welcomed her like she was a familiar hostage. Empty, she sat.

And waited.

FLORIDA

. . .

THAT NIGHT, IN FLORIDA, an elderly woman arrived home from her church group and reached into her refrigerator for a strawberry and banana yogurt. This one was her favorite flavor. Not because the taste or texture was the most appealing. It was because this is the flavor she'd introduced her grandson to long ago—so her grandson thought it was her favorite flavor. He grew up thinking that. So it became his favorite flavor.

She smiled, inside and out, thinking about that.

She loves her grandson. He loves his Nana.

Her reliable old Zenith was showing the news. Some brief story, barely half a minute, of some "American service members" (whatever that means) "killed in a training exercise in Jordan."

The news is always so depressing. She turned it off and stepped down into her glassed-in breakfast room to enjoy her late-night snack.

She heard an owl.

THE BROKEN MAN

...

THE MAN SCREAMED IN pain.

Only torture sessions could be this bad. If only the rest of the world had ever endured—no, endured is the wrong word to use, no one can actually endure a severe torture—or experienced real torture by professionals, then nobody would be as arrogantly brash about their own hypothetical response.

This isn't like in the movies where, strapped to a chair, the hero says, "I'll never tell you anything," between his screams or instead quips clever wisecracks. When it's real, there is no portion of the brain capable of wisecracks.

Even in training, it is always the brashest, toughest alpha who cracks first. The jock-type tough guy who predicts, "Not me!" Always.

If one ran a clock on them, the it's-not-me tough guys are always the first ones who jabber away (if you don't count the rat weasels who never even make it to the actual physical torture part before they start ratting). The second group, surprisingly, are the hyper-intellectuals who, through clenched teeth, try outsmarting or dealing with their torturers.

It is an odd statistical phenomenon that the least

information and longer wait to get it, generally comes from those who are considered physically the weakest—women, children, and frail men.

This is due to several factors. One is that those who fit that description are more mentally and emotionally bound to their emotional ties (personal loyalties, other family friends) and higher consideration for others within their social network is harder to break than the alpha-types for whom such social considerations are but secondary anyway. The weaker people generally live their lives with more adherence to that and greater caring for others, thus stronger loyalty is a natural part of their relationships.

Another reason of this counter-intuitive phenomenon is that this type of person is not accustomed to combat. And torture is a form of unfair combat. It is a second nature of this type to not try to fight things they encounter and are well-practiced and experienced in resolving that the other side will win because they always do. This expectation of loss leads to a hopelessness and despair, which allows for a greater tolerance of pain and discomfort, since they're used to it.

A third reason that this type is typically last to give up the goods is simply because they blubber so hard that their speech isn't even comprehensible to themselves (in fact, the torturers often have to stop frequently, or slow down to translate).

But, no matter what, everyone cracks eventually.

Everyone.

So this is why CSTs are taught (or used to be, who knows what kind of training it is these days now that the contract facilities and specialized camps have taken over) that at the breaking point, you must reveal something. Not anything crucial, really, just something the torturers don't know. Give them some real rabbit to chase—just not the critically vital rabbit.

It buys time at least.

But still, the torturers may come back. They may go harder. And again, eventually everyone cracks. Everyone.

Especially when they get to the breaking of bones part.

The man who screamed out did so almost in anger that he was in such pain. He knew, without hearing any official diagnosis, he was broken. His bones were. Some of those bones were critical ones.

It made him angry that of all the ones he knew were broken, it was his right leg which was the most painful. Agony combined with anger.

He counted the separate pains.

Left lower ribs. At least two broken.

Right thumb.

Right hand.

Nose. Badly.

Right big toe (though hard to tell, since it's so cold).

Left upper temporal area, skull.

Lower right leg. Probably mid-fibula.

Right ankle.

And a tooth.

Anger and agony.

It made him angry that he'd allowed himself to be put into this position. This situation must have been preventable. Guilt flowed in.

Somehow, somewhere, he must have screwed up.

Just like always.

Inattention.

Somewhere along the line, there had to have been some sign, some way to notice, predict such an outcome, then prevent it.

This always friggin' happens.

Just when things look to work out how it was planned, he does something to screw it up—or, more accurately, he *doesn't* do something, which screws things up.

So the moral is, if you find yourself brutally tortured, it's your own fault. That's not exactly healthy self-talk, but people in this line of work aren't exactly mentally healthy. No sane person would do this.

Nevertheless, he knew he had to find a way out of this, despite the fact that he knew he was now a cripple.

He had to turn this around on the torturers.

The first thing he needed was to get an understanding of his surroundings. It was pitch black. Darker in here than he'd ever experienced. Cold.

Especially his right toes (if they were still there).

Very little noise. Air rushing through a vent.

Yes. He could feel it on his face.

His face. He could feel that it wasn't 'moving' properly. Probably swollen or disfigured in some way.

But, the air on it was cool.

Not the back of his head, though. It was sweating. As was his back. He thought he heard a passing jet engine. Near an airport?

But nothing else.

Nothing.

But pain and anger.

His face wrestled with itself a bit more.

The man opened his resisting eyes.

Well, that explained the total darkness. He should have tried that before. He opened them slowly. It took great effort, as he didn't want to alert the torturers that he was awake.

Torturers don't torture sleeping people do they? The room wasn't bright at all. Moon-lit, really. Or cityscape-lit perhaps?

White acoustic tiles as a ceiling. So, not a cave or basement. Some sort of official building.

The man pitched his eyes around the room more boldly, seeking any sign of a presence and getting a feel of the room itself. Roughly 10' x 14' or so. Fluorescent lights flush with the ceiling tiles. No sign of anyone.

Time to chance moving his head.

Hmm. This looks like a standard private hospital room.

This was even a metal-frame, railed bed.

That is not good. He knew what happens in hospitals.

Or, what *could* happen.

Or, what *did* happen.

Wait—does torture happen in hospital rooms?

On hospital beds?

Not yet feeling he could lift his head, he brought his left arm up near his face as his eyes squinted. A simple hospital band on his left wrist. After a moment, the dim light revealed, hand-written, the name Keith Smith. But it showed no other information at all, including location.

"Okay," the man said, with a bit of relief.

It was written in English, not Arabic. And, he wasn't shackled to the bed. Curling up a bit, he saw he was alone.

Time to examine himself. His right hand was in a

hard-shelled air cast, velcroed tight, immobilizing the limb from his knuckles to his elbow. It was tightest on the hand. Only his thumb, probably also broken, had any independent range of motion. The gauze sticking out from underneath the air cast on the top of his right hand indicated that he'd had an ORIF to one or more of the carpels. Who knows what hardware had been installed in there. It wouldn't be the first time, actually.

His right leg was in a cast from knee to toes, which were blue as they protruded from a leg elevated on a pillow.

Do torturers use stacks of fluffy-white clean pillows?

Maybe the smart ones do.

No, that's probably not right.

There probably weren't any torturers responsible for this.

At least, not the pillow part anyway.

Somehow, he found all this disappointing. Inexplicable, really. But maybe he felt he deserved angry torturers instead of fluffy white pillows.

No, that's just his guilt talking again. Or, his shame for screwing things up.

Plans, even the perfect ones, require perfect execution.

Like a complex recipe.

This is why professional chefs are the ones best qualified to follow a recipe to its perfect conclusion. Often, even the tiniest procedural deviance results in catastrophic failure.

This was obviously a catastrophic failure for the Broken Man.

No, not catastrophic. Catastrophic actually would involve a cave with a blood-thirsty, vengeful torturer.

But still a failure.

Not many could relate to this, but that really was a strange comfort. He was comfortable with failure. It was familiar ground to him.

Maybe that's why he was usually so intense. Push. Push. Push. Success and victory were the only acceptable goals. Failure is a powerful motivator. Being on top demands staying there. That's much harder to do.

But, maybe that's also why he historically allowed his inattention or complacency to sabotage his successes. Whenever he did find himself on top, it was uncomfortable for him. Being the winner, the 1st place guy, the grand champion, felt wrong. As if it had to be some sort of accident. Like someone else deserved the gold medal—not someone more worthy of it, but someone who was part of the club.

The Broken Man wasn't really the join-our-club type. He was the kind of guy who'd always made his own club. A new club that was better than the other more established yet inferior one.

The problem is, that is *not* the path of least resistance.

That's how one ends up in trouble with the established orthodoxy. The 'established' have always awarded themselves such power as to make things difficult, even survival, for any arrogant upstart.

And the 'arrogant' label is almost always flung about at the upstarts. For any new innovation is but a rejection of the establishment, is arrogance—how dare Mr. Edison think to usurp the long-established lamp oil institution.

Arrogance is bold. Arrogance is confidence. Arrogance is empowering. It is only a negative if it is unearned. Earning it requires certainty. Mozart's arrogance allowed his drive, his motivation, to rise to his level of talent. It is also what allowed him to mind his weaknesses so as to strengthen them.

False arrogance ignores that. It allows one to be blind to their weaknesses, which could be completely exploited. That reveals the arrogance to have been unearned. Less sophisticated thinkers often label this phenomenon as 'blinded by arrogance.'

No. That is a false arrogance. A meaningless bluster. A façade worn by someone who is inattentive to some weakness, inherent or not.

The real failure is that inattention. Ignoring a tiny detail can lead to catastrophic failure.

There it is again.

Thoughts in a loop. It happens when weakened so bad that the only strength left is reserved for suppressing the pain.

Thoughts in a loop.

It went on for maybe hours (though in this mental fog, it might have only been minutes).

Then there was the heavy-looking wooden door to his right. At his two o'clock. The latch noise proceeded the inward swing toward the far wall, allowing the Broken Man but a brief glimpse into the space beyond. A hallway, probably. Then an arm appeared. The arm became a person, blocking his view of the hallway.

A small middle-aged man with a slightly oversized nose and severe frontal receding baldness entered. Military-style uniform. The man looked at the Broken Man without hesitation, as if familiar, as he closed the door before taking a few steps toward the bed.

Broken Man needed a moment to process that this was

a real person and was really happening, not a mirage of the brain fog.

The military man needed no such time and went about inspecting the supine Broken Man, beginning at the purple toes (while frowning) and ending at the man's left (anterior) temporal wound to the head.

"These staples should come out tomorrow," he said. "Dr. Pinkney has already signed off on it."

The military man's inspection was as casual as looking over a just-washed Buick.

"Staples?" Broken Man managed to ask. His left hand, the uninjured one, slowly rose, shaking to his head to touch the gauze where his hair was supposed to be.

"Yes. Staples," the military man repeated as he returned his attention to the toes, even squeezing one to note the capillary refill response time. "I'll probably do it myself. First thing in the morning, if that's ok with you? So you can shower in the orthobath."

"Orthobath?" the Broken Man was perplexed.

"Yes," the military man tapped the right leg cast with an ink pen. "You got maybe another week in this, so you can't get it wet."

"Um—" Broken Man struggled, embarrassed. "Why am I here?"

The small man shrugged as he scribbled onto a small notepad. "You're not ready to be released yet. Still a couple X-rays from being cleared. We don't know how well your hand is going to take. We haven't determined if your nausea is reaction from the pain meds or TBI, possible concussion. I say likely. You still experiencing vertigo?"

"Vertigo?" the Broken Man asked. "When did I have that?"

The small man's eyes locked onto Broken Man's. "Seriously?"

The Broken Man sat agape, not knowing what to say. He glanced at the small man's name tag—Hassan.

Hassan tucked the small notepad away. Left pants pocket. A lefty. Small fingers. His wedding bad was an ill fit. "Your last episode was just this morning when we picked your ass up off that floor! You aren't cleared to walk until we clear you to walk. Understood? If you need to go potty, use the bedpan as instructed. If you cannot figure out how to use that piece of sophisticated hardware, then push that damn button (pointing) and a private can be summoned to hold your privates! Got it, Mr. Smith?"

Yes, this guy is definitely military. Arrogant prick.

"My name's not Smith," Broken Man replied. "I didn't mean *why am I still here?* I'd like to know what caused me to be here. And—well—where *is* here? And how'd I get here?" He noted the eagle insignia and added, "Specialist Hassan?"

Hassan sighed and shook his head. "This is like the tenth time you've tried to pull me into that conversation. It won't work. What I can answer is that it is my job as a PA to tend to Dr. Pinkney's patients. You are in that bed. That makes you a patient. Your injuries are my responsibility, and that's all. You show up here, in this room, you get treated, Mr. Smith. But, if you want my opinion, since you're asking—again—as to how you came to be in this condition, I can only assume that you and your fellow 'diplomats'—if they really are that— probably injured yourselves after slipping on a carpeted floor where you'd spilt your caramel latte. Or you got tangled in a fax machine cord while trying to have phone sex with an answering machine. Or a stapler in your office went rogue as you tried to unjam it. Maybe you all went on a tour in your Vespas and couldn't figure out which key to insert to operate the brakes?"

An Air Force PA deriding someone like this? Are you kidding me?

"I just—don't remember—*how* I got here—last thing I recall was—" Then he stopped. It's definitely not something he could talk about.

"I remember," Hassan's eyes narrowed, "your ass on this floor this morning as you puked on my shoes. I remember throwing them away. I remember having to borrow a pair of shoes from someone else. Good way to contract toenail fungus. Hard to get rid of that."

Threw up on his shoes—ah, okay, got it. That explains the hostility. Well, some of it anyway. The rest is just typical DOD bullshit. Particularly those within the 'officer's corp.' Assholes. The Broken Man hoped he hadn't said all of that out loud. He hadn't, though. Too complicated for the brain fog. What he'd actually said aloud was, "Oh. I'm sorry about your shoes. I—I just didn't know—"

Hassan huffed, "That's exactly what you said this morning. Listen, I highly recommend you clean up as soon as I get your staples out in the morning. You're a mess and one of your managers is scheduled to come see you before lunch. Probably to fire you for fucking up the stapler or fax machine or Vespa or whatever you broke. I remind you, again, there are strict orders for you not to contact anyone, not to leave this room for any reason and, like I read to you before, these orders have been issued down with such a force that they must come from very high. You, Mr. Smith, are officially not even here. I can assume you really pissed off some ambassador's wife or something."

"I—I don't remember you telling me that. Thank you."

Hassan shook his head again as he angled toward the door. "As for me, I personally think you are probably OGA"—which is common DOD parlance for CIA—"because you just don't know shit!"

And with that, Hassan was gone.

Good riddance.

Still, 'Keith Smith' sat there, surrounded by his brain fog, answerless.

As he drifted into slumber, no answers came.

Not that he could remember anyway.

OPERATION RECOVERY

. . .

THE ANSWERS CAME THE next day, as Keith's 'manager' walked into the same room to discover a freshly showered (half-assed) Keith trying to scratch underneath his cast.

"I don't think you are supposed to do that."

Keith looked up at the man blankly for a moment. The brain fog had lifted a bit, but his thoughts were sluggish. The recognition did come, but it was slow.

"You're definitely not as well-dressed as the last time I saw you. Or even the time before that."

The man wore a zip-up one-piece jumpsuit, of the kind often worn by train mechanics with near-permanent grease under their nails. When in Rome…

"Where are my guys?" Broken Man asked the new-comer.

"What guys?" the new-comer returned. "There are no guys."

"C'mon, man," Keith pushed. "I need to know."

The response came quick. "No. There is no 'need to know,' because there are no guys. There never were any."

"But, listen—"

"But nothing," the 'mechanic' raised his palms. "If you're asking about a few of the patients who were admitted about the same time as you, then they are all alive. Some wounded like you. One blinded in one eye. A couple others got hardly a scratch. Aside from the semi-blindness, it looks like you caught the worst of whatever happened to you. A couple have already been released. One of them was concerned about you. Wanted to see you."

Just one?

"Mr. Smith, it is not really my business how you came to be at this hospital in Germany. I have no information for you. I can only surmise that the roof you fell from was high and steep. It also looks like you hit quite a few tree limbs on the way down. Painful. But if not for those limbs, you might have been even worse. Maybe taking a job with a German telecom isn't for you. Perhaps you should return to the States and try something safer. Like being a tax preparer or graphic designer. As for patients visiting other patients, well, that would be an irregular occurrence. That's not a normal thing, is it, Mr. Smith?"

"Wait a minute," Keith shook his head to clear the cobwebs. "Am I being shut out of my own operation here? That information is being sequestered? From me?!?"

"Nothing is being sequestered, Mr. Smith. There was no operation to sequester."

"Then why are *you* here if not to coordinate a formal debriefing?"

"I am *not* here. And there is nothing to debrief. Nothing happened."

Keith shook his head. "Wait—just—wait a minute," his face scrunched and his air-casted right hand went to his temple. "You don't understand. There—there's going to be a debris field. I need to know how we—I made it from the crash to here—"

"There was no crash."

"Listen! And—and who discovered us? Who was notified? Who was mobilized? I need to know who was involved, seen, contacted."

"So that *what*? So you can contact them? Create more interest? More of a trail? No. Things which don't happen, Mr. Smith, cannot be investigated can they? It only brings attention. Is that optimal?"

"People will ask questions. Make connections to what happened. They'll come after those involved and you know it."

"Those who were suspected to be directly involved, if such people exist, are now dead. They all died in a helicopter crash. A cover-up of the cover-up is already underway. An operation to make it look as if a country is covering that up."

"A red-herring cover-up?!?"

"Exactly. But you don't need to know about that, Mr. Smith, because you couldn't have been the least bit involved with those dead men—since you were too busy falling off a roof. Those men, if they ever existed, died. Dead end. There is no vengeance for anyone to extract against someone who's already dead, is there? The story, which doesn't exist, ends there. Any aliases used by such nonexistent men are necessarily dead. The entire world, if anyone is interested, thinks they are dead. The reality is that you actually were dead, considered as such, anyway. Everyone thought so, except a couple. So that part was easy. Everyone still thinks so."

Dead. Darn. It was a shame—that was a well-liked cover.

"But you still don't understand," Keith persisted. "I need to debrief—"

"There will be no debriefing. There is nothing to debrief, since nothing ha—"

"So I get that we were collected. Or somehow collected ourselves. But there was a cell phone. Was it left behind? Was it collected too?"

"Cell phone?" the man's eyes went wide.

"Yes."

There was a long pause while the man processed that information. "When I met you in Tennessee, you told me everything you'd need. I made sure you had it. A cell phone that you'd leave behind wasn't one of them."

"Neither was a helicopter. We had to change the plan."

"You mean you had to improvise. That doesn't sound like you."

"We were left no choice. This is why you need to know what went wrong and what we all had to do to—"

"No—I don't need to know anything. Neither does anyone else. Ever. That would be a bad, bad, bad idea. It's over. Leave it that way. Still, the cell phone bothers me. There was no mention of it. Does it lead back to any of our people?"

"Not directly. But to someone in my network, it does. I was using it to indicate each checkpoint. He was supposed to update Mike each step. Especially the last one."

The man's eyes closed as he inhaled deeply. "Not good— but there's nothing you can do about it now. Except play dead. By the way, your career is dead, too. OSA is officially closed for business. Yours was the last contract and that ended a month ago. I'm stepping aside. This was my finale. Thanks for that."

"What? Am I persona non grata now? You can't step aside. You can't close up shop," Keith said. Left unsaid was that he really was in a tough spot financially and that this was a bad time to lose opportunities.

"What? Your satellite business? You think you can start producing again with that telemetry gig you're working? Well, you'll have to find an agency sponsor to put you in a green jacket again. Because I'm out. After today, none of you will ever see me again. Hell, I'm not even here now."

'Keith Smith' shrugged. "Well, I always thought Jody could step up and, y'know, take the reins, if need be."

"Shit," the man scoffed. "Jody's as tired of all this as I am. Maybe more. So good luck with that, Mr... SMITH." He left with a nod.

Keith Smith. New cover. A temp job, really. Just long enough to recover well enough to leave this place without asking—or raising—any questions.

Let Operation Recovery commence.

Maybe Keith Smith could find a way to pull this off without screwing it up.

Probably not.

DEATH OR PRISON

...

THE PHYSICAL RECOVERY FOR Keith Smith spanned just over 10 weeks, enough time for November to arrive. The rest would be healing and physical rehabilitation on Keith's part to return to whatever level of fitness he could.

By the time Keith Smith boarded the plane in Germany, landed in New York, then D.C., then took a cab to a particular used car lot to purchase a green convertible Chrysler LeBaron (as someone named 'Rett James') then drove it the familiar interstate (I-40) home, a lot had changed.

He still had not thought of a way to explain why his three-week vacation had lasted three months (actually spanning across four calendar months), why he'd be using a crutch or a cane, and why he was driving yet another new (used, really) car home.

That last part he worried about because Anita had already told him he had too many. He knew she'd make him sell the Fiero and the Blazer, but maybe she'd let him keep this convertible. Women like convertibles, right? (He already knew the answer to that—women only like convertibles for themselves. They don't like their man in a convertible.)

But, if it came down to it, he'd sell this one too, leaving only the Cherokee—if that'd help him woo her back.

As it turned out, that was starting to look like a longshot. Almost as soon as Anita returned from Louisville from watching over Rett's hospitalized grandfather (long story), her own multimillionaire father had indeed taken her house shopping. Rett's absence had allowed Anita's father the opportunity to regain his daughter, and so he seized it. The closing on the new house was, in fact, this week.

To try to win her back, Rett would capitulate to her every demand, hoping to counterbalance an outburst he'd had which had accelerated their fissure in the first place, no matter how irrational her demands were.

She wanted two more dogs to keep Bear (their Great Pyrenees) happy, so they got two more dogs. She named the shih tzus Peppe and Raisin. Rett didn't remember Bear asking for new company, but he acquiesced, hoping against hope he was finally able to do something right. Besides, the less stress at home the better, since he was already stressed beyond his capacity. His business was still failing and his absence at a critical time hadn't helped. He wasn't training, which was a major stressor, since the only reason he'd even considered Tupelo in the first place was because that was the only city around with a black belt of high enough rank to train someone of Rett's rank.

Plus, there was a new stress that Rett had not ever encountered before—so he couldn't identify it until it had taken root. Like Mississippi kudzu, it crept into his metal landscape and because (in part) he'd had little experience with it, it began to seize control. He began looking over his shoulder. All times. All places. Nothing was safe anymore.

Paranoia is not a mental disorder. It is a mental state. It is properly characterized as maladaptive if there is no cause for it. And to any person outside of one who feels it, it must be that there's no cause ("Stop it! No one's out to get you.").

That is easy for them to say. Others.

But those others simply don't know because cause is not written within their realm of experience. Imagine how silly it would be to tell a bank robber in his getaway vehicle, "Hey you! Stop stressing and being paranoid. No one's after you!" Or, saying the same thing to an entrenched soldier in the middle of a battle.

Sometimes the paranoia is justified. There is cause for it. You cannot seek or get therapy for it because the therapist simply cannot relate. It is outside of their experience because they have no cause. So they project that standard onto others, even when those others *do* have cause.

Paranoia, the earned and justified kind, at least, is a very cold thing. It is like the frozen vacuum of space and is relentless in its attack. Imagine feeling like the getaway bank robber or cornered soldier—but all the time. Constantly.

This is why Rett really needed more closeness from those around him, not less. He tried to invite Anita to Thanksgiving at his mother's ancient home in Meridian. It didn't help (although his mother was happy he was actually alive).

Just after that, she moved all her things and herself to her new house, leaving Rett alone in his big house on George Avenue. Well, not entirely alone. She left him with the two dogs—the ones only she wanted—and his beloved cat Victoria, who was happy to be reunited after the Thanksgiving retrieval.

She took only Bear (which also turned out to be only temporary).

Rett still persisted, even as his business was falling apart around him. He asked her on dates. She'd accept. They went to Nashville to see Diana Krall, one of Rett's favorite singers, in concert.

But nothing was there.

Anita had already pulled away.

All that was left was that cold paranoia.

As Rett tried to limp through dark days. Literally.

Some stories have happy endings. Real life doesn't.

But it does give you chances. More chances even after disasters and destruction. Because, the reality is that real stories don't end. Life keeps giving you chances to change it. To add to it. The story doesn't actually end. Until you die.

Rett had already done that.

Cradled to his chest, he took his young shih tzu, Peppe, out to the side lawn and lay down in the grass on a cool night. He could see Christmas lights blinking in the neighborhood on the other side of the creek. Victoria sashayed across the lawn from who knows where and joined Rett and the playful pup.

Rett sighed as he looked up at the sky. Slowly, more points of light came into focus. Out of instinct, he started scanning for low-earth-orbit satellites. His phone buzzed from his pocket. Peppe was hardly interested as Rett answered it, "DST."

"Oh," the female voice said in a soft, but sultry way. "I was just going to leave you a message. Merry Christmas."

He responded, "Merry Christmas to you, Nikki. I was just thinking about you."

"No you weren't. You were probably thinking about Dana." Dana was Rett's kryptonite. "But I appreciate the compliment."

"I want nothing but the best for you, Nikki. I need you to know that."

"It's not your job to take care of me, Rett. It's *my* job. You take care of you now. You hear me?"

"Yes, ma'am. I do."

"You'll find a way to land on your feet. You always do. Or get back on them."

Rett sighed. "This has been a pretty big fall from grace, Nikki. No matter what I've done—for—everybody, it doesn't matter."

Trying to allay his concerns, she softened. "Well, it could be worse. The path you've chosen often either ends in death or prison. And you haven't had those. So, it could be worse."

She was wrong about that. Dead wrong.

Rett just shook his head. He hadn't told her all of it. She didn't know.

"It's all gone. Gone or going away. Everything. Money. Wife. Even you, Nikki."

"So what's your Christmas wish?" she asked.

Rett looked up at the stars. "To start over. Find a way and—start fresh."

"Okay then," she replied. "Good night, Rett. Merry Christmas."

"Merry Christmas."

Rett re-pocketed the phone and pet Peppe, still lying on his chest. He refocused on the shining dots. Thinking about starting over.

One dim dot caught his attention. For a moment, the cold paranoia vanished.

He squinted at the dot. It was moving. A single point of light, elusive, but there.

He smiled.

"Got you!"

AUTHOR'S NOTE

Dear reader,

If you picked up this book expecting the typical fun and zany misadventures of Rett James that you've come to expect from the spy-com series *The Beancounter Saga* that are the B.B. Quincy books, then I apologize for the dramatic departure that is this one.

While I've found it healthy (perhaps some coping mechanism) to deal with things with humor, I've also noticed that writing events with the solemnity that they are due is also an important part of my corpus of catharsis. Some things are too serious, too affective, and too weighty to find any comedy in whatsoever.

I envy those who have lived a life full of the frivolity of a new puppy.

I haven't.

I don't know that there's a lot of entertainment value in darkness or in the sharing of it. I suppose there is, though; a lot of people love mystery or horror movies. I don't. That's not entertainment for me—too much like real life. I don't know what your preferred escape is, but the story told in this very book, I suspect, will be easy for you to put down once you are done with it. When you are finished with it, you can set it up on a shelf and get on with your life.

I haven't been able to do that. I'm never done with it, it seems. I hope one day I can be, because the story you hold in your hands, in these pages, won't let go of me. Since I didn't know what else to do, I wrote it down. For just over two decades now, people who don't or can't understand have advised me, "Just let it go." But again, I state flatly, I'm *not* holding onto *it*. *It* is holding onto me. Anyway, life isn't always happy and bouncy. If there is a lesson here, there may be two:

1. I don't recall if this came from Nietzsche or not, but paraphrasing—"Be careful spending your life doing battle against every monster you see, lest you become one."

2. When surrounded by darkness, every pinpoint of light, no matter how fleeting, is to be cherished.

J. Everett Dutschke

ABOUT THE AUTHOR

J. Everett Dutschke is absolutely no stranger to controversy and has never been afraid to tackle even the most difficult, perhaps even hopeless, missions. In addition to multiple other highly praised books, he penned *The Beancounter Saga* of the B. B. Quincy spy-com series (sequels to this book) which are also based on true events.

Though prominently featured in many newspapers and magazines around the world, movies, books and even a television series, Everett still prefers a much more simple life—simply sitting and playing guitar or thinking for hours on end.

Currently, he lives and works in a high-security government complex, contemplating the next big project.

OTHER BOOKS BY
J. EVERETT DUTSCHKE

The Perfect Weapon

How God Does It

Eggshell Expression

B.B. Quincy and the Giant Kraken

B.B. Quincy and the Minotaur

B.B. Quincy and the Green Dragon

B.B. Quincy and the Cyclops